TANA HOFF

A BOY NAMED

Joshua

A STORY OF BELONGING

A BOY NAMED JOSHUA
Copyright © 2022 by Tana Hoff

Scripture quotations are taken from the Holy Bible, New Living Translation, copyright ©1996, 2004, 2007 by Tyndale House Foundation. Used by permission of Tyndale House Publishers, Inc., Carol Stream, Illinois 60188. All rights reserved.

This is a work of fiction. Names, characters, places and incidents either are the product of the author's imagination or are used fictitiously, and any resemblance to actual persons, living or dead, businesses, companies, events, or locales is entirely coincidental.

The content of this publication is based on actual events. Names may have been changed to protect individual privacy.

ISBN: 978-1-4866-2319-8
eBook ISBN: 978-1-4866-2320-4

Word Alive Press
119 De Baets Street Winnipeg, MB R2J 3R9
www.wordalivepress.ca

WORD ALIVE
—P R E S S—

Cataloguing in Publication information can be obtained from Library and Archives Canada.

This book is dedicated to our beloved Isaiah,
whose unique and lovable ingenuity was my inspiration.
Also, a big shout out to foster moms and dads. God bless you all.

CONTENTS

INTRODUCTION

SOME BELIEVE THAT the best way to overcome deep pain is to help others. The "why me?" mentality pops up over and over again in our minds. However, when we take our minds off ourselves, we realize we're not the only ones living with hurt. As Jonathan Decker, clinical director of Your Family Expert and family therapist, states, "This ubiquitous cry of the suffering displays an urgent craving for answers. Those best qualified to assist a suffering soul are those who have passed through similar ordeals."[1]

My husband and I began attending a new church in our city at a point in our lives when we felt like we were drowning in an ocean of hurt, confusion, and loss. We looked forward to the lively weekly worship with fellow believers. We found hope in the meaningful and relevant messages in the sermons each week. Often, guest speakers spoke about seeking the light during times of darkness, or their journey of serving the Lord. Many stories conveyed human trials of pain and suffering, some of finding peace, and others who were still searching for repose.

One Sunday morning, a young lady spoke about fostering children. She talked about the forever-growing need for foster families in our small city. This included her own experiences fostering children, as well as the importance of including the child's biological family in the process. She inspired us to become foster parents, something I never dreamed that my husband and I would become. Our own children were grown adults, the youngest in post-secondary school, living at home at the time. But, a few years after that talk, a four-year-old boy became part of our family.

This book is the story of one little boy. It is a fictional story based on life experiences. The names and characters may sound familiar, but they have been changed to protect the privacy of characters represented in the story. The intention and purpose of this

---

[1] Jonathan Decker, "The Secret Way Suffering Helps Us to Help Others," Your Family Expert, August 28, 2015, https://yourfamilyexpert.com/how-suffering-helps-us-to-help-others/.

story is to share the unpredictable and profound daily life of genuine incidents, ongoing circumstances, and common occurrences within a foster family. They progressively result in forming unique and, perhaps uncommon, friendships between strangers, who are meshed together through one little boy and his journey of belonging.

PROLOGUE
July 2020

"HEY, MAC," I called from the second level loft as he walked through the front door. "I just received a text from Joshua's mom. She was just released from the hospital after spending two weeks battling pneumonia. She's moved to a women's shelter with the kids, they are hoping to return home soon. Joshua is asking her if he can come and visit us." I hustled down the stairs to join him at the front entrance.

"Sure, what happened?" he replied, hanging up his denim jacket.

I crossed my arms. "I don't know the whole story, but it sounds like a difficult situation. In any case, after being confined at home all winter because of COVID-19 safety regulations, and now living in the small space at the shelter, I'm certain Joshua would probably enjoy a week at the cottage. Some fun in the sun and outdoor scenery change will do him good."

"Yeah, I agree. It'd be great to have him visit."

"I'll let her know!"

I returned to my desk in the loft, where I'd left my phone, and sent Miranda a text message right away: *Hi, Miranda, we can pick Joshua up Monday around supper time. I can pick up some clothes for him to wear while he stays with us at the beach for the week.*

She responded, *Thank you, he's very excited. The shelter has been hard on him. He doesn't understand why we had to leave our house.*

I sent back, *No worries, see you soon!*

PART ONE
Before Joshua

CHAPTER ONE
A New Job

EARLY MAY BROUGHT warm weather to our small fair city of Rockport. The lustreless months of winter and dull dark mornings faded as the trees started to bud and the sun peeked out a bit earlier each morning.

It was humid in the large gymnasium where we gathered as a church to worship each Sunday morning. My mind was far away from the physical presence of my body, my mind occupied by heavy thoughts. I needed a change in my work place. More than twenty years of teaching and working for Sunstone Park Elementary brought security, yet discomfort, equally. My soul was burdened by the contemporary changes my traditional school division was making.

Church gatherings always uplifted me. We had been attending this particular church for over three years, and the worship and pastoral teams always inspired me to "keep on."

As I browsed through the church bulletin, I noticed a small advertisement at the bottom of the page: *Rockport Christian Academy is looking to hire a kindergarten teacher. Please call the church office for more information.* I just about knocked my husband, Mac, off his chair with my elbow after reading the job notification.

I barely slept a wink that night. My plan was to call the school church office immediately the following morning to find out more about the kindergarten position. After hours of tossing and turning, sleep finally found me, and I awoke with a sense of excitement and grogginess. I proceeded with my morning routine with feelings of hope and curiosity.

As soon as I arrived at school, I closed my classroom door and made the call, leaving a voicemail. By morning recess, the principal had returned my call and scheduled an interview for a couple of days later. By noon, I was beside myself with anticipation. Though I texted Mac, who responded with encouragement, I needed to tell someone face to face. Off I went to talk with a trusted colleague, and she responded with surprise and enthusiasm.

Within two weeks, I had accepted a one-year temporary teaching position with the Christian Academy. I took a leap of faith, put my trust in God, and resigned from my permanent position of twenty-seven years.

The long process of packing up a lifetime of work began. I spent early mornings boxing up materials, recycling items, and getting rid of outdated resources. I was thankful I was a spring cleaner and hadn't held on to too many extra materials from my teaching career.

The first week of packing went well. However, I realized I was going to need a lot more time to complete everything on my list before the end of June. Packing up my classroom became less of a concern as year-end responsibilities grew closer, like writing report cards and meeting paperwork deadlines, which needed to be finalized by the end of June. To make room in my schedule, my morning run and daily devotional reading took the hit, and my Bible remained opened on the upper counter of my kitchen island.

I'll just get back to the page where I left off, as soon as report cards are complete, I thought as I slid it over to the far-left side without closing it.

As for my morning run, the only energy I had left was at the end of the day for a short walk around my neighbourhood to help me to calm my anxieties about the "new" to come.

––––––––––

Over the past few months, Mac and I had been taking a course on becoming foster parents. We were inspired to learn more about fostering through a guest speaker and member of our church who spoke about her experiences one Sunday morning. However, not long after we started the course, the Institute of Child Services began ameliorating the child welfare and protective services department, and our case worker was transferred to another department. This process of completing our course, which should have been done by May, lingered throughout the year.

While we waited for a new case worker, our lives became busier, with travelling to visit Mac's family in another county and my new job change. Though Mac and I continued to attend group training sessions and complete essential assignments required after each topic was covered, we had begun to let them slide. Without a case worker to submit them to, we lost interest in doing them. Both of us were mentally and physically exhausted from our weekly work routines and busy weekends. We were, however, still very interested in fostering a child. My course binder sat with my still-open Bible on the kitchen island. One day I would slide both that binder and my Bible back to front and centre.

"Hey, Sara," Mac walked into the kitchen one evening in the middle of a particularly busy week. He poured himself a glass of sweet tea. I lifted my head from the report card I was going over and looked up at him. "We've been so busy lately. How about we head out to the cottage on Saturday morning and spend the weekend relaxing? We could put the dock in the water and enjoy a couple of days away from the city. Maybe even cut the grass, as I'm sure it's needing some TLC."

I responded with mild enthusiasm, "Sure, a short peaceful cottage visit would be nice." I glanced at the stack of report cards on the kitchen table—just a few more to proofread. I thought about Mac's suggestion and decided a beach getaway was just what we needed.

One night in mid-June, not long after our beach weekend retreat, a phone call caught me off guard. I was inside my walk-in closet picking out a comfortable outfit to wear to school the next day. I hurried over to the nightstand for my phone and answered the call. I didn't recognize the phone number, and I was curious as to who the caller could be.

"Hi, is this Sara Jamison?" said the voice on the other end.

"Yes," I said.

"I'm Jackie with the Institute of Child Services. I have you on a list as a possible foster family home."

"Oh, yeah. Yes!"

"We have a four-year-old boy needing a placement. His current foster home is unable to care for him. Are you and your husband interested in fostering a child this young? He needs to be placed as soon as possible."

My mouth gaped. I hadn't expected this call so soon. "Uh... I will need to talk with my husband and daughter. Your phone call has caught me by surprise!"

"Of course, take a bit of time to think it over and discuss it with your family. Please let me know before the end of June. If you have questions, let me know."

"What's his name?" I asked.

"Joshua."

"What a nice name! I'll get back to you before the end of June."

I hung up the phone, a thousand more questions flooding my mind. I stood still, thinking and processing the call until my husband's voice broke the silence.

"Who was that?" he asked, perhaps prompted by the stunned look on my face.

After discussing the call as a family, we decided to move forward and complete our course work, and the next couple of weeks saw us racing through the homework we'd left unfinished. Night after night, we met with a worker to get caught up on our assignments, just in case we took in this little boy named Joshua. Tess, our youngest, was completely on board with the idea of having a younger foster sibling join the family. She thought it would be cool to be the big sister. Her words stuck in my mind like glue.

"That would be awesome! I've always been the youngest in the family. I'm not home a lot, but I can help out occasionally," she said, reminding me that she was a young adult with plans and a future of her own.

Before the last day of June, I once again, found myself tossing and turning through the night. Both Mac and I had demanding jobs. I was in the middle of changing schools, and Mac travelled short distances around the county, tending to a variety of projects. After the well celebrated July national holiday, I would be busy emptying the kindergarten room at the academy to prepare it for painting. I wondered if I'd have the energy to tackle this job immediately after cleaning out my classroom at Sunstone Park Elementary.

Unable to sleep, I prayed, "Lord give me the strength, guidance, and wisdom for the challenges and decisions that need to be worked out and finalized by tomorrow and days following."

My mind flipped back and forth through my final day at Sunstone Park Elementary and my mental list of jobs to do concerning my new classroom, as well as thoughts about fostering a child. I asked God, "What do we do about Joshua?"

My brain still unable to turn off, I decided to get up. It was around midnight; the house was silent. Feeling a bit hungry, I decided to warm up some leftover dill and potato soup. As I sat at the kitchen island, savouring that delicious blend of dill and potatoes, I saw my Bible laying open on the counter. I realized I had neglected my daily devotional readings for quite some time, and this would be the perfect opportunity to pick up where I had left off. I reached over and slid my Bible in front of me, still open to the page I had left off at in May. I couldn't believe my eyes: the first page of the book of Joshua lay open before me. This was a clear and definite sign from God: Joshua was to join our family.

After only a few hours of broken sleep, I awoke eager to talk with Mac about accepting Joshua as our foster son. At breakfast I showed him my Bible, explaining my midnight encounter with the Lord.

Mac listened carefully, cupping his hand under his chin in contemplation. He responded, "Oh wow! I agree. God is pointing us in the direction to give this young fellow a family and home."

"Okay then. I'll call the social worker after school today and inform her about our decision," I said.

CHAPTER TWO
Phone Calls That Change Lives

I WASN'T SURE whether it was the exhaustion and lack of sleep, or the fact that I was staring at my empty classroom where I had worked many of my career years, that left me hollow inside. Sunstone Park Elementary had been my home for so long. The final day of school seemed to move along quickly, but periodic moments lingered in my mind, bringing back a lifetime of memories. The clock on the wall with its quiet ticking broke the silence in the room. At three o'clock, the end of my day, I finally let some tears leak from my eyes. Before I left permanently, I took a long glance at my classroom as I closed the door quietly.

My drive home from school that day was soundless. My body hummed with tension and my thoughts slowly changed from an ache to anticipation as I neared my home, thinking about the phone call I was about to make to the Institute of Child Services.

Once inside, my heart pounded as I dialed the phone number in front of me. A voice answered on the third ring.

"Hello, Jackie speaking."

"Hi, Jackie, it's Sara Jamison. We spoke a couple of weeks ago concerning fostering a boy named Joshua," I said.

"Hi, yes, thanks for getting back to me," Jackie said.

"Mac and I, as well as our daughter Tess, have decided to welcome this little boy into our family if his situation is still the same."

"Oh, wonderful! Yes, his living arrangements are the same as the last time we spoke. I'm so glad you're opening your home to him. The family he's with is anxiously awaiting news of his transfer. I'll give you their phone number and you can arrange a pre-visit with them. We'll take care of the paper work on our side. A case worker will need to meet with you next week to finalize the details."

"Great! I'll give the family a call tonight."

We said our goodbyes, and I hung up the phone.

Later that night, I made the phone call to the Taylors, the couple currently caring for Joshua. We arranged a pre-visit at a park near their home for the next evening. It was the July holiday weekend, and we would have a short visit with them before heading out to the cottage.

———————

Mac slowly and skilfully manoeuvred the fully-loaded and packed-up truck into a tight parking space parallel to the playground. I glanced around the crowded park, my eyes roving over the play structure and pathways. Families were out by the dozens, enjoying the warm summer evening. We walked a few paces with Piper, our fourteen-year-old Jack Russel dog, watching for a couple our age with a little boy.

I smiled at Mac and spoke with excitement and curiosity in my voice, "I wonder what Joshua looks like?"

"We'll soon find out," Mac responded evenly.

They came upon us by surprise: a robust little boy on a training bike, a man with slightly greying hair of average height, and a woman of a shorter stature and short-cropped hair, all smiling. The woman held out her hand to shake Mac's and my hands as she introduced herself and the others.

"Hi, we saw you pull up and park your truck. By the way you were looking around the park and the description you gave of yourselves over the phone, we guessed who you were. I'm Jan. This is Steve, my husband, and this little fellow is Joshua."

I pulled my hand back. "Hi! I'm Sara. This is my husband, Mac, and Piper, our dog."

After greeting each other, we walked around the park, Joshua showing off his bike skills and keeping a curious eye on us. As far as he knew, we were Jan and Steve's "new friends." Occasionally, he would call out to Jan and Steve, "Nanny, Pops, watch me!" as he proudly manoeuvred his bike up and down slopes and around curves during our walk. I couldn't help but be drawn to this little boy, with his big dark eyes and eyebrows that would tilt to match his facial expressions.

As we drove away from that first meeting, with the understanding that we would have a follow-up visit at our house soon, I felt my heart flutter. I already loved Joshua.

Mac looked at me, "You know, it's a big responsibility!" he said.

"I know."

Silence followed for the next hour as we drove to our cottage, Mac and I sitting in quiet contemplation.

I broke the silence first, just as Mac began the steep descent down the hill to the resort. "My main concern is whether or not we will have the energy to parent a preschool-aged child. I've been thinking about all of the activities and early childhood stages we went through with our own children. I'm hesitant, but my heart is full of love for Joshua, even after a short visit with him."

Mac responded calmly with a few collected thoughts. "I agree. Let's just enjoy the weekend and see how the next visit goes. Joshua is on my heart as well."

———————

The widely-celebrated July holiday weekend brought excitement and life to the peaceful resort where our cottage was located. There was much to do to prepare for the summer months. We woke up early Sunday morning planning to launch our boat and two jet skis. The boat launch was extremely busy with weekenders and residents eagerly waiting their turn to do the same. The lake was like a sheet of glass, perfect for launching. Mac backed the truck and trailer down the concrete pad and launched the boat quickly. Once the boat was in the water, we cruised along at a sprightly speed and relished in the breeze stirred up by the movement.

Mac exclaimed with a loud voice, "This is so refreshing!"

I nodded my head in agreement. We zipped up and down the busy lake for a while and then pulled up to our dock.

"It's going to be a hot and sticky day," Mac said as we covered the boat.

"Yup, I can feel the mugginess in the air," I responded.

We walked up the stairs to our deck. I grabbed a couple of water bottles from the fridge in the cottage and gave one to Mac. He was looking towards the lake.

"Let's get the jet skis in the water as soon as possible," Mac suggested, as he made his way up the stairs to the garage.

I quickly followed behind him, and we launched both jet skis without delay. The wind had picked up, causing small white-capping waves. We enjoyed plowing through the water at high speeds, causing both of us to be thoroughly drenched, the perfect cool-down for the heat of the day!

The following Monday morning, I planned the upcoming week over a second cup of coffee. I quickly realized that this summer would not be one of rest, relaxation, rejuvenation, and leisure. For the next three days, I'd be cleaning up my new classroom and dealing with inspections to get our home ready for Joshua. Contractors would be performing checks and reviews needed for the furnace, fireplace, and safety devices, such as the smoke alarm and carbon monoxide detector, to ensure a safe environment for a foster child.

Next, I called Jan and Steve to set up a time for Joshua to visit with Mac and me at our house, leaving a message when the call went to her voicemail.

I would have never imagined that the phone calls I made over the past few weeks would change so many lives in the future to come.

CHAPTER THREE:
work to DO

DRESSED IN RUNNING pants and a tank top, I headed out the door, but not for a run—I was to begin the task of emptying my new classroom and sorting its contents.

It was just after ten o'clock in the morning. The kindergarten room was dark and quiet, and the smells of the last day of school lingered in the air. I opened the door to the classroom slowly, flipped on the light switch, and peered around the room, taking in the clutter. Oh my, there was work to do! Excitement trickled through my body, though I also felt overwhelmed. I didn't know where to start. After looking around for a moment, I decided it best to make five piles: one for garbage, one for recycling, one for charity, one for keeping, and one for items I was unsure about what I was going to do with them.

I began toiling through the classroom. The school was still, as the teaching staff had left for the summer. The only sound I heard in the distance was the clamouring of construction from the other side of the school where renovations were underway. The day was unending, although I cleared heaps of items out of the classroom, the space appeared to be as bestrewn as ever.

By six o'clock, my stomach growled with hunger pains. I had only furrowed through one quarter of the room, and I realized that the next two days would be long and exhausting. I would need to begin much earlier and stay later to get through it all. As I took one last glance around the class room, I decided it best to recruit a little help from Mac. I most definitely had underestimated the time it would take to sort through and organize classroom contents, as well as empty and prepare the room for painting.

Upon arriving home, I noticed Mac's work truck in the driveway, indicating he'd be off to work again soon; he only brought it home when he was called out of the city to fix a problem after regular work hours.

"How was your day?" he greeted me as I walked through the door.

I was too tired to talk, so I just shook my head.

After changing my clothes, I headed to the kitchen to make supper: something lighter, since it was already after seven o'clock.

As I was clumsily moving around cooking pots in the cupboard, looking for a smaller one needed to make our supper, I barely heard Mac's voice calling me from the upstairs loft, "By the way, there's a voicemail on the answering machine from Jan, something about bringing Joshua for a visit sometime this week."

I dropped the lid from one of the pots in my hand, startling Piper, who was napping by the back deck door in the kitchen. I'd forgotten about the visit. I quickly called Jan back, and we planned our visit for Friday evening.

Mac and I gobbled down a pot of macaroni, and then, exhausted from the day's events, I crashed for the night while Mac left for work, hoping to return by midnight.

The next morning, I opened my eyes, trying to focus on the fuzzy red numbers on my clock radio. It took a few seconds for seven-ten to come into focus. Mac was bustling about the bedroom, almost ready to leave for work.

"What time are you going to work in your classroom?" he asked me.

I jumped out of bed, my eyes wide, thinking it was a school work day with students. I quickly realized that I had planned to get an early start cleaning the remainder of the classroom. I calmed down and thought to myself, *Oh my, how could I not have remembered!* "I was aiming for eight o'clock this morning," I said.

I started pulling clothes from my dresser when I remembered that I needed some help and muscle power assistance to move some of the larger items in the classroom. "Mac, do you think you can stop in after work today and help me with a few things?" I asked.

"As long as I don't have any emergencies at work, I can be there by five-thirty," he said, as he pulled on his t-shirt and grabbed his denim jacket from the chair in the corner of the bedroom.

"Thanks. I'll only need your help for about an hour."

Mac kissed me as he left, and I quickly dressed. Then I grabbed my water bottle and snack to take with me and hurried quietly out the door, so as not to wake Tess, who was sound asleep from a busy night at work. *It might not be as quiet in our house once Joshua moves in*, I thought in the spur of the moment.

The next couple of days passed quickly as I finished emptying out my classroom. The maintenance staff would be painting the shelves a neutral colour, and the painter would give the walls a much-needed fresher upper coat of white. The school administrator had ordered four round child-sized tables and a circle-time carpet decorated with the alphabet. I was so thankful to everyone for their help with renewing the kindergarten classroom for the upcoming school year. My heart filled with a sense of satisfaction and content. I couldn't wait to start the new school year.

PART TWO

Life with Joshua

CHAPTER FOUR
New Beginnings

THE DAY OF our follow-up visit with Joshua was busy, as I went shopping to pick up a few items for the spare room; it needed a few things to make it warm and welcoming for Joshua.

Jan and Steve were planning on bringing most of Joshua's belongings in the evening, and he would officially move in the next afternoon. Jan mentioned to Mac and me that they had told Joshua that he would be spending some time with us. He had lived with Jan and Steve on and off since he was a baby, and they didn't want him to feel abandoned by them, or be afraid that he wouldn't see them again. They were informed that permanency plans were being made for Joshua and his siblings. Though biological family visits had occurred once a month previously, they had now ceased due to a variety of issues. At this point, Joshua would be categorized as a long-term placement until he was eighteen. Permanency could possibly lead to adoption, but this had not been decided as of yet.

Before they arrived, I changed the quilt on the guest room bed with one that looked like race car stripes. I propped up a brand-new stuffed animal in front of the pillows and hung pictures of two of Mac's favourite race cars—a Shelby Mustang GT500 and a Ford Mustang Mach 1—as well as a set of three colourful pictures from the movie *Cars* on the walls. My heart beat with excitement as I transformed the guest room into a suitable space for a little boy.

When the doorbell rang twice, I opened the front door to welcome our guests. After touring our home, Steve retrieved Joshua's belongings from their vehicle and placed them in his bedroom. Joshua seemed confused and unsure of this transfer of his "stuff." His eyebrows tilted and he blurted out, "Why did you bring all my toys and clothes here?"

We distracted him with a lively game of air hockey in our basement recreation room. Joshua stood on a chair at one end of the adult-sized air hockey table so he could see over the top and squealed with delight as he smashed the red puck around the table. He couldn't get enough! Just before eight o'clock, we sat down at the kitchen table for a light snack of cookies and milk, as well as coffee for the adults, and Joshua seemed to forget about his treasured belongings in the guest room. By eight-fifteen, the Taylors and Joshua left as quickly as they had arrived.

The next morning, I carefully unpacked Joshua's clothing and personal items, organizing them into the empty dresser and closet. Jan and Steve had provided Joshua with quality books and toys, and cute but durable clothing; I wondered how they would deal with him no longer being in their home, as they seemed to love him a lot. I knew it would take some time for Joshua to become familiar and comfortable with his new home, and it would also take time for us to get to know each other. However, we planned to keep in touch with the Taylors.

The doorbell rang at exactly two o'clock. There stood Jan and Joshua, Joshua preoccupied with pushing the doorbell over and over again and Jan obviously holding back tears. Jan handed over a list of Joshua's food likes and dislikes, as well as the information for his health care providers and the names of his biological siblings and parents. Then, she gave Joshua a big hug and kiss and left quickly and quietly.

Joshua looked up at us, his eyes big and sad, and asked, "When is Nanny coming back to get me?"

We were not prepared for this question. As a teacher, I was often surprised by the sensitive and sometimes difficult questions asked by my students. I would distract them by bringing up a topic that was light and fun to talk about. I would answer their challenging questions once I had time to think about and process how to handle those unique issues.

I raised an eyebrow at Mac, indicating he needed to support my response to Joshua. "I have a great idea," I responded with enthusiasm. "We can go out to our cottage tomorrow and go for a boat ride. We can take a picture of you driving the boat and send it to Nanny and Pops!"

"I don't know how to drive a boat," Joshua said, his voice wavering with uncertainty.

Mac intervened, "I can show you. We can both drive the boat together."

With that, we showed Joshua around his new home. Joshua slowly peeked into his room and then carefully looked in each dresser drawer, finding his belongings and clothing. Next, he opened the closet door to find his toys in a bucket and the rest of his clothes hanging neatly from the closet rod. Satisfied that all of his precious belongings were safe and sound, he brightened up a bit and asked for a snack.

As we walked down the hallway toward the kitchen Joshua pointed to the closed door and asked, "Whose room is this?"

I responded enthusiastically, "That's our daughter Tess's room. She's at work, but you'll meet her soon enough."

Once in the kitchen, Joshua went directly to the refrigerator and opened the door; he certainly wasn't shy about food! He selected an orange and devoured it. Then he opened the pantry door and spotted the Bear Paw cookies.

"Can I have a Bear Paw please? Nanny always let me have one."

"Yes, you can, thank you for asking so politely!" I replied.

While watching Joshua, I noticed that he was a tidy eater. He took small bites and chewed his food slowly. After the snack, Joshua washed his hands at the kitchen sink. Standing on his tiptoes, he soaped up his fingers and quite enjoyed this task.

"This soap smells good!" he said.

I was a huge fan of enticing soap fragrances, and I knew Joshua would soon discover that every sink in the house had a hand soap with a fresh fragrance.

"What can we do now?" Joshua asked.

"How about we go outside and you can ride your bike around the bay for a while?" Mac suggested.

Joshua's bike was leaning up against the side of the garage, close to the front door. Joshua seemed surprised to see it.

"What's this doing here?" he asked.

Mac responded, "We can put it in the garage together after you are done riding it."

"But it's supposed to be at Nanny and Pops' house."

"I think they left it here for you to use while you stay with us. You can show us what a good rider you are," I said.

Mac helped Joshua put his helmet on, then Joshua rode his bike around the island in the middle of the bay. It was very quiet, as most of the neighbours were tucked away in their houses or away on summer vacations. This left for an open area on the road without cars as obstacles: perfect for a four-year-old learning to balance on a bike.

While Mac and Joshua played outside, I went back inside the house and packed a few items for our trip to the cottage planned for the next day. After packing, I made supper: sausage, perogies, and creamed corn, a simple meal that was both filling and delicious. It was also, according to Jan, Joshua's favourite. I opened the front door and called the boys for supper, remembering when my own children were playing outside with their friends. There was one significant difference, though: my own children came in the house after the first request. Joshua needed a bit of persuading, to say the least. We were learning a great deal about him in the four short hours that had passed.

After supper, Mac and I used a tag team parenting approach to help Joshua with his bedtime routine. Mac helped Joshua brush his teeth and wash his face in the washroom. I joined Joshua in his bedroom to help him put on his pyjamas, read a couple of bedtime stories, and say a prayer.

Before climbing into bed, Joshua pointed to the race car pictures on the wall and asked, "Whose cars are those?"

I lifted Joshua up onto the bed and drew the blankets over him. "Mac used to have a car similar to the ones that you see on the wall, the other cartoon pictures are from a kids movie," I said.

As I turned out the lights, Joshua spoke up with a tremor in his voice.

"Can you leave the light on?" he said.

The light switch had a dimmer feature, so I turned the light back on and lowered the brightness.

I was about to close the bedroom door when Joshua's voice piped up once again. "Can you leave the door open?"

After one more hug, I left the door partially open and said, "Goodnight."

I found Mac, head bobbing in his chair, at the kitchen table. I tapped him on the shoulder, hoping not to startle him.

"Mac, I'm calling it a night, it's probably a good idea for both of us to get some sleep while Joshua is asleep. I have a feeling that we'll have a night of interruptions."

Sure enough, much later, both of us were sound asleep when we awoke to a voice calling out in terror, "No, no!" followed by some indistinguishable mumbling.

Mac and I jumped out of bed, looking at each other, realizing that Joshua was having a night terror. We darted down the hallway to Joshua's bedroom and found him sitting up, completely asleep, screaming out words that were distorted and unclear. I walked over to him and quietly said, "You're safe Joshua, go back to sleep."

As we settled back into bed, Mac reminded me that Jan had said that sometimes Joshua would awake or have bad dreams after biological family visits, or drastic changes in his living arrangements. Thankfully, Joshua had calmed down and fallen back asleep almost immediately. But it wasn't so easy for Mac, who was a little shaken by the sudden awakening. After tossing and turning for a while, sleep overtook us both.

Once again, I was startled from my deep sleep. Standing two inches from my face was Joshua, quietly looking at me.

"Is it time to get up yet?" he said with a happy voice as I opened my eyes wider.

I glanced at the clock radio; the red numbers said that it was six o'clock in the morning. "Almost," I said. "Go back to bed for a bit longer, and I'll come and get you when I get up."

Off he ran down the hall, and I heard him climbing back into bed. Next, Joshua began to sing nursery rhymes. I soon learned that this was his coping strategy for easing his anxiety when going to sleep at night, waking up in the middle of the night, or waking a little too early in the morning.

After about twenty minutes of staring at the ceiling, I decided that a cup of coffee and early start to the day was needed. I slipped on my housecoat and started down the hall. Suddenly, the sound of feet thudding against the hardwood floor resounded from Joshua's room. He greeted me half way down the hallway with a smile and a panicked foot dance.

"I have to pee!" he said.

I headed for the kitchen to make breakfast and a pot of coffee, the sound of water running in the main bathroom indicated Joshua was washing has hands. I listened for a bit then decided to check on him, as the water seemed to be running for longer than I anticipated. Sure enough, there Joshua stood scrubbing his little hands, face, and arms! The smell of the fragrant soap once again had him enjoying this necessary routine. I adjusted the water pressure to a slow flow and convinced him to rinse the soap off and dry his hands.

Just then, Tess opened her bedroom door and startled Joshua. He quickly darted behind me, peering at Tess.

Tess smiled at Joshua and said, "I can still see you! What's your name?"

Joshua formed a smile and told Tess his name. Then he asked, "What's your name?"

She responded with "Tess" and asked Joshua if he was finished in the bathroom.

He responded wisely, "Yup, remember to wash your hands!"

Tess laughed and said, "I will!"

After a breakfast of cereal, a banana, and a glass of orange juice, we got ready for the day and packed a cooler with sandwiches and fresh fruit for our trip to the cottage. We couldn't wait to get Joshua out on the boat!

CHAPTER FIVE
sunny Days

THE SUN WAS out in full force! We could feel its warmth on our faces as we stepped out the front door around ten-o-clock in the morning. It was going to be a hot day and we were looking forward to spending time at the cottage. The seventy-five minute drive to our summer abode passed by quickly! Joshua dozed off fifteen minutes into the drive. We drove in silence until we reached the turn off of the main highway. Joshua perked up as we descended down the steep road toward the lake. He kept his attention on the magnificent turquoise colour of the water and seemingly unending length of the lake. As we drove down the steep slope, the decline made it look like the road disappeared into the lake.

"Are we going to drive into the lake?" Joshua asked with curiosity and excitement.

"No, it's just perspective," I answered.

"What's perspective?"

"It's how you view or see things."

My answer seemed to suffice; however, Joshua kept his eyes on the road ahead, leaning forward in his car seat, quietly waiting with anticipation to see what would happen. Mac slowly drove down the hill so that Joshua could take it all in, and to avoid hitting any wildlife such as deer that would unexpectedly dash across the road! Once at the bottom of the hill, Joshua sat back in his car seat with a sigh of relief! Mac made a right turn at the fork in the road and followed the elevation of the winding, paved roadway until we reached our destination ten minutes later. He steered the truck down the gravel pressed driveway and parked the truck. Joshua's eyes widened as he spotted the large play structure, tree-house and sandbox, all of which Mac had built for own children when they were little.

As soon as he was out of the truck, Joshua ran to the play structure, climbed the tree house, and slid down the big yellow slide. Mac and I laughed as we opened the cottage and set out the umbrella and chairs on the deck. Piper bolted for the dock and frantically barked at us, wanting us to join her for a swim: her favourite activity. She loved to run as fast as she could toward the end of the dock and leap into the water. She would dog paddle her way back to shore and repeat the process. Memories of when our children were younger flooded my thoughts. Piper would enthusiastically swim out to the kids as they floated on inner tubes or flutter boards. She would try to climb upon the flotation devices, and our kids would call out with frustration, "Piper's bugging us!" Poor Piper, she was just joining in the fun!

Mac joined Piper down at the dock and uncovered the boat. Joshua was feeling the sweltering heat, so we headed inside for lunch. Joshua was fascinated with the cottage's upper loft. He stood stoically looking out the front windows, which reached from the bottom to the top of the thirty-foot wall, and excitedly pointed out all the boats and watercraft on the lake.

"Come on, let's wash up for lunch," I said.

"What are we having?" asked Joshua.

"Sandwiches and fruit." I had some popsicles in the freezer that I would surprise Joshua with after our anticipated boat ride.

I showed Joshua how to wash up in the bathroom sink. We had to fill the sink one quarter of the way with warm water, soap up, and rinse with the tap on very low flow to conserve water usage and prevent the septic tank from filling up too quickly. Once again, Joshua inhaled the fragrant soap.

"What's this smell?" he asked.

"The fragrance is called 'Ocean,'" I responded.

After a quick lunch, Mac headed down to the dock to lower the boat into the water while I fitted Joshua with a life jacket from our equipment shed. Located down a stone path to the right of the cottage, the cedar shed was once a child's play house, but now we used it to store our outdoor equipment: life jackets of different sizes, water skis, wake board, fishing rods and supplies, paddles, and other sports equipment and toys.

Joshua squirmed as I tightened the life jacket on him, feeling hot in the sun. I reassured him that, once we were out on the lake, the breeze would cool him down. We made our way down to the dock, where Mac was waiting in the boat for us. Joshua had never been on a boat before, and he slowly stepped onto it, clutching the side as it careened and leaned from the weight of each passenger. Once we were seated comfortably, Mac backed the boat out and then steered to wide open waters. He gradually accelerated the boat, pushing forward on the throttle, which caused the bow of the boat to point upward at an angle. Joshua squeezed my wrist tightly, but, once the boat levelled off and we sped down the lake, free as a bird, a cheek-to-cheek grin crossed Joshua's face. He had no words. His eyebrows shot up like Spock's from *Star Trek* when Mac asked if he would like to help steer the boat. I snapped a photo of this brave venture and sent it to Nanny and Pops at Joshua's request.

Moments later, I received a response from Jan: *Looks like he's having fun and becoming comfortable with you both!*

Jan and Steve loved Joshua immensely. They missed him dearly, and Mac and I knew it was heartbreaking for them to have to let him go.

On hot weather days, we often anchored the boat and dove off of the boat's back deck to cool off. Joshua would have no part in this! He sat, content to watch us while we swam and cooled down, though we did convince him to sit on the ladder and put his feet in the water. After a ten-minute splash, we climbed back into the boat and headed back to the dock.

For the rest of the afternoon, Joshua played on the dock with a net and pail, trying to scoop up the little minnows that would scurry in schools past the dock. Mac and I covered the boat and then sat on the dock bench, watching Joshua bend over the dock, determined to catch as many fish as possible. We left his life jacket on just in case he tumbled forward into the water.

Every ten seconds he would call out, "Look!" as he dumped his minnows into a plastic pail.

He was insistent about bringing his catch back to the sandbox, where he could keep an eye on the little minnows. Mac tried to convince him that it would be best to release them back into the lake, however Joshua disagreed.

He was so enthralled with fishing that we promised he could catch fish all summer long. We would even get him a fishing rod. I made note to pick up a child's fishing rod so Joshua could practice casting. This helped to persuade Joshua to dump the minnows back in the lake before we returned to the city.

As I prepared supper, Mac checked the boat and hung up the life jackets. Joshua played in the sandbox, forming roads through the sand to push the toy dump truck through.

I poked my head out of the front deck door to call the boys in. "It's time to wash up for supper!"

Mac called back, "Okay, give us five minutes!"

I watched as Mac tried to teach Joshua how to lift himself up onto the swing. Joshua was struggling, so Mac lifted him up and placed him carefully in the centre of the U-shaped swing. Mac gave Joshua a few gentle pushes, and it was nice to see a wide smile appear across Joshua's face. I could hear Mac encouraging Joshua, "Good job!"

After a supper of barbecued hamburgers, we drove back to the city. Joshua slept all the way back home. He awoke as Mac pulled into the driveway and turned off the ignition, silencing the hum of the motor. Joshua spoke softly with a groggy voice, "Where are we?"

"Back in the city," I replied.

"Are Nanny and Pops here to get me?"

Mac intervened, "It's late. I'll carry you into the house."

Joshua clung tightly to Mac, tucking his head into Mac's shoulder. My heart ached for Joshua. He clearly had deep feelings for Jan and Steve.

Once inside, we managed to get him through a quick bath and a few spoonfuls of Rice Krispies. The snap, crackle, and pop of the cereal was no match for Joshua's weariness, and his head bobbed over his bowl of cereal. Mac quickly picked him up and tucked him into bed. He was out like a light! We had tuckered him out at the cottage.

CHAPTER SIX
A Day in the Life On the Bay

THE NEXT MORNING, we were up and at it before nine o'clock. While Mac went to work, Joshua and I headed out into the bay to take Piper for a walk.

Oh my, this is going to be a long and very warm and muggy day, I thought as we crossed the street and walked toward the park with a small play structure.

Joshua ran directly to the swings. I helped him on to the swing, then gave him a couple of pushes. I tried to explain how to "pump" with his legs to go higher, but the concept didn't seem to register with him.

Next, we walked along the path through the park and back home. Watering the flowers kept Joshua busy for almost an hour while he filled the watering can and gave each flower pot plenty of water.

After gulping down a large glass of water, Joshua rode his bike around the island of the bay. Round and round he went, often calling out, "Sara, watch me!"

"Good job!" I called back.

It was nearing noon and the bay was quiet. There was no sign of life, human or animal. The few children who resided in the bay were perhaps away on vacation or avoiding the heat by staying indoors. I was hoping that Joshua would have the opportunity to meet the girl who lived next door to us, but maybe another time.

Joshua called out again, "I'm hungry!" So, we headed inside, where I made him a ham sandwich for lunch.

During lunch, Joshua asked, "Can I watch 'Treehouse' after lunch?" while munching on his sandwich.

"Do you mean that you would like to play in a tree house?" I asked, taking a bite of my own sandwich.

"No, it's on TV!" Joshua said.

"Oh, a television program," I said.

"No, it has *Max & Ruby*, *Toopy and Binoo*, *Blaze and the Monster Machines*..." Joshua said. "I watched it at Nanny and Pops.'"

I thought about this for a moment. My own children didn't watch a lot of television, so I didn't know much about current programs. We made our way downstairs where the basement was cool and comfy. Joshua snuggled beside me as I surfed through channels to find his request. I was surprised to find how many children's channels there were. It had been over fifteen years since programs like this had crossed the screen in our house. I quickly found the Treehouse station and checked out the shows. After finding that the shows seemed innocent and child-friendly, I left Joshua with a warm fleece blanket and pillow and allowed him to watch two programs while I went back upstairs and started preparing dinner.

When I went back downstairs to check on Joshua, I found him asleep half sitting up. Of course, as soon as I turned off the television he woke up and groggily asked, "What are we going to do now?"

"How about I pull out some of the toys my kids used to play with when they were your age?" I responded.

He seemed to perk up at that. "Where are the toys?"

I pointed towards a door. "They're stored in the back room in a closet, here in the basement. We kept some of their favourites."

Joshua jumped off the couch and enthusiastically opened the back room door. When he found the closet, his eyes glazed over the toys neatly stored on the shelves: buckets of Lego, Bionicles, a medieval castle, a large bucket of dinosaurs, a doll house, a large bucket of toy vehicles, a bucket of Hot Wheels cars, and puzzles and games. Joshua immediately chose the Hot Wheels. On the way back to the recreation room, we passed by the room where I was storing my school supplies. Joshua peeked in, his curiosity evident.

"What's all that stuff?" he asked.

"That's my school stuff," I said. "I'm a teacher. I'm going to take those things to my new school next month. You can come along and help me organize my classroom if you'd like."

His eyebrows furrowed, indicating he didn't quite understand. Joshua hadn't even been to preschool yet, so the concepts of school and classroom were new. I realized I'd have to look into preschool classes and part-time childcare for him as well.

Joshua became engrossed with playing with the Hot Wheels, making car sounds and squeal noises while pushing them around. He collected his favourite colours and models of the cars and lined them up, which gave me an opportunity to put my teacher hat on.

"Joshua, can you count the cars you have lined up?" I asked.

He immediately began counting, "One, two, three," all the way up to eleven successfully, but then had trouble with the bigger numbers. "Thirteen, thirteen, fifteen, nineteen."

Not bad for a start. We would definitely work on counting. What a coincidence that I had a basement full of educational activities I could put to good use over the summer! Next, we both sorted the cars by colour and made a parking lot for each group. This time when I asked Joshua to count the colours, he was not as cooperative. I soon learned that, when an activity required Joshua to think and focus, he very conveniently changed the conversation, a coping skill I recognized in children who struggled with attention.

When Joshua became bored of the cars, he asked, "Sara, can I pick another toy from the closet?"

"How about we choose some puzzles and take them upstairs for you to play with while I set the table for supper?" I replied.

Joshua chose a few puzzles and sat at the kitchen island, talking to me and trying to fit the puzzle pieces into place. I saw that he forced the pieces together when they wouldn't easily fit with each other, so I sat beside him and showed him how to find the edge pieces first. Next, we pieced the frame of the puzzle together. The puzzle had twenty-four medium sized pieces, so it wasn't overly difficult, but Joshua needed a few instructions on how to finish it. I explained how to figure out where each piece might fit by looking for matching colours and markings. Finally, we fitted the final few pieces into the middle of the puzzle. Joshua was overwhelmed. He sighed and asked for a snack. We peeled two large oranges and devoured each half-moon piece with delight.

Mac would be home from work soon, the chili simmering on the stove, and the garlic naan only needed to be warmed up before serving. Joshua stood in the hallway to the living room. He looked at me, then at my piano.

"Can I play the piano?" he asked.

"Yes, you can, but you need to play it gently. My piano is very precious; my mom and dad gave it to me," I said as I showed him how to press down on the ivory keys and the black sharp and flat keys.

I left him to explore, experiment, and enjoy the sounds of the piano. I could hear him quite clearly tapping away on the keys from the kitchen, where I was writing a list of items we needed for our next weekend beach trip.

Just then, Mac walked in the front door. Piper bounced up and down happily, the noise from the piano stopped, and I greeted Mac with a very genuine, "I'm so glad you're home!"

Mac tilted his head in a questioning motion.

"Where were you so long?" Joshua blurted out as he ran to the door.

"I was working," Mac replied.

Joshua grabbed Mac around the legs and hugged him fervently. I remembered that Jan had remarked that Joshua needed a strong male role model in his life. Steve provided that critical relationship when Joshua was part of their family. Mac peeled Joshua's arms away from his knees and showed him how to do a fist bump.

"Let's wash up for supper!" I said.

Joshua watched as I filled a glass bowl with chili and pressed a tightly fitting lid on top. He asked, "Who's that for?"

"It's for Tess. She's working and won't be home for supper, so I'm saving her some for later," I answered in a matter-of-fact tone.

His next question caught me off guard, but it was so sweet. "Do you think she'll play cars with me?"

I looked at him and nodded my head. "You can ask her when you see her."

Joshua looked at me intently and responded, "But I hardly ever see her."

"I know, me too!" I said.

After dinner, Mac and Joshua went outside. This was routine for Mac, as he had many chores to do and garage projects on the go: tuning car engines, fixing motor bikes, and rebuilding anything motorized. He was a perfectionist when it came to cutting and trimming the grass, and he spent extra time making sure it looked well-groomed and lush. He routinely and graciously watered my droopy, water-starved flowers. Tonight, however, he was planning on washing the truck. Mac gave Joshua a pair of big rubber boots to wear, followed by the water hose with an attached brush for soaping and scrubbing the mud off of the truck. Mac showed Joshua how to clean every nook and cranny. Joshua also washed his bike, then polished the tires just like Mac had done to the truck tires. I glanced out of the front door an hour later and watched Joshua ride his balance bike around the island of the bay. The bike looked small for Joshua: his knees were bent at an angle and his feet dragged along the road. Mac and I would need to purchase a bike for Joshua that matched his height. Children grow like weeds!

Going outside after supper became part of Mac and Joshua's regular routine. Joshua always looked forward to working on special jobs before bedtime.

CHAPTER SEVEN
Day by Day

THE FOLLOWING DAYS passed by much the same. Joshua and I continued with our outdoor routine in the morning. We walked the dog, played at the park, and watered the flowers. I continued to encourage Joshua to work on puzzles while I made lunch, and promised him his own Hot Wheels car for each completed puzzle. He would be able to have a car collection of his own if he was willing to keep going.

One day, we took a shopping trip to find him a pair of water shoes for the beach and a child's fishing rod. The one we found was just the right size for a him, and it came with a plastic hook and a lure that was shaped like a fish. Joshua reminded me about the three puzzles he completed and my promise to purchase a car, so we stopped by the toy department and he selected three cars. He was so thrilled with his rewards that he tore the packages open as soon as we settled into our car. I listened to the sound of car noises the entire drive home. We were slowly becoming comfortable with each other.

Of course, we encountered some bumps along the way. One night, after supper, Mac and Joshua went to the garage and vacuumed the inside of the truck. Mac had an air freshener hanging from his mirror, and Joshua noticed this immediately. Mac explained that it made the inside of the truck smell clean, like it would smell if it was brand new.

Joshua took a big whiff of the freshener. "It smells good! Can I have one for my bike?" he asked.

"You don't need one for your bike," Mac responded.

"Why not?"

"It's not made to freshen up the outside air."

"Can I have one anyway?" Joshua pleaded. "I want my bike to be like your truck!"

Mac was amused with Joshua's comment. "Alright then, let's see what we can do," he said, smiling at Joshua and giving him a fist bump. Mac proceeded to hang a green air freshener, shaped like a tree and smelling like pine, onto the handlebars of Joshua's bike. "There you go, buddy!"

Joshua was so proud of it that he took to the bay immediately to ride his bike and show off his new "bike freshener." The hour outside quickly passed, and soon it was time for Joshua to begin his bedtime routine. I called out the front door, but there was no response.

A minute later, Mac ventured up the walkway with frustration in his voice, "He's not listening to me. Can you come and get him?"

"Where is he?" I asked.

"On the corner of the bay, sitting on his bike."

I slid on a pair of flip flops and walked toward Joshua, a neutral expression fixed on my face. He returned my gaze wide-eyed. He knew he was in trouble for something, he just couldn't figure out what it was.

I approached Joshua cautiously and asked him why he was refusing to listen to Mac when asked to come into the house. Joshua began to stammer and cry at the same time. Finally he managed to say, "I want to keep riding my bike!"

"You need to come inside the house now. It's getting dark outside and it's almost time to for bed. I am going to count to three. If you are not moving toward the house when I start counting, there will be consequences," I said softly, but with authority in my voice.

Joshua looked at me inquisitively, and then almost in a panicked mode, headed toward the house. I'm sure he didn't understand the word "consequences," but my matter-of-fact tone quickly prompted him to listen. Once inside the house, I asked him to apologize to Mac for his belligerence. He did this solemnly, though once again I wasn't sure he understood what the word "belligerence" meant because he tilted his head and said, "Is belligerence good or bad?"

I knelt down, looked into Joshua's eyes, and spoke calmly. "It means that you were rude."

After Joshua went to bed, Mac and I sat at the kitchen table, too tired to move. It had been a while since we had a little person living in our home. Mac was disillusioned.

"I asked Joshua three times to park his bike in the garage and come in the house with me. We were getting along fine, he was happy with his air freshener, and I was delighted that he was enjoying our time together," he explained.

"Cheer up! It's been a while since we've parented little ones," I said. "We overcame so many challenges with our own children as they were growing up. The only difference is that we were much younger then. We're just getting to know Joshua. I'm sure we'll figure what strategies will work to get him to comply the first time around to simple requests."

My words didn't seem to comfort Mac, but, he did agree with my comments. As Mac got up from his chair, I patted his back and said, "I think Joshua is very fond of you. All kids push the limits, and Joshua will test us at times, but we'll get through it."

————————————

Once the weekend hit, we were off to the lake again. Our daughter Tess and her boyfriend Tydon were planning to visit with us at the cottage, and we were looking forward to seeing them both. Tydon had a three-hour drive from where he lived in Foxpine, then Tess and Tydon would drive the hour and a bit to the cottage together. They would arrive later in the afternoon.

On our way out, we made a detour to a town thirty minutes south of our resort to look at a bicycle for Joshua. It was located in a scenic valley, making it challenging for Joshua to manage the sloped street when he tried out the bike. He used his tiptoes to manoeuvre his way a short distance and he appeared to be hesitant to use the pedals. Joshua squinted his eyes and commented, "This is too hard."

Mac grabbed onto the back of the bike seat to hold Joshua steady and said, "I've got you." Joshua looked back at Mac and smiled. We purchased the bike for Joshua and continued on with our drive to the cottage.

Once settled in at the cottage, we headed for the dock. Joshua seemed content to walk along the shore in his new water shoes with a net and pail looking for treasures. I sat back in one of the Adirondack chairs watching people fly by on wake boards, skis, and speedboats, their joyous screams and laughter echoing across the lake.

"Hey, Mom and Dad, we're here!" a voice called from the cottage deck. Tess and Tydon had arrived.

Mac, Joshua, and I made our way up to the cottage. We walked up to the cottage deck to greet Tess and Ty, hugging them tightly. It was so nice to have them with us for the weekend; they both worked a lot and, between taking turns travelling back and forth to see each other on weekends, we rarely saw them. Joshua watched the affectionate greeting with cautious curiosity, his eyes wide open and his body frozen like a statue. When Tydon said "Hi," Joshua scrambled behind Mac, clutching his legs.

Mac reached for Joshua's hand, and we made our way inside the cottage. Joshua needed time to warm up to Tydon. Tess smiled at Joshua and asked if he would like to come along and help her show Tydon around the cottage yard. Joshua jumped up as quick as a rabbit and grabbed Tess's hand.

We spent the afternoon on the dock, enjoying the beautiful sunny weather and calm breeze, swimming in the lake, catching up, and eating snacks.

Around six o'clock, Tess, Joshua, and myself headed up to the cottage to change out of our swimsuits into dry clothes. I made supper and Tess and Joshua set the table. Tess and Joshua then went back down to the dock to let Mac and Tydon know that supper would be served in fifteen minutes. Not long after that, I heard footsteps on the deck and the back door opening. In walked Tess and Joshua, both soaking wet from head to toe.

"What happened?" I asked. After inspecting Joshua for any scrapes or bruises, I was relieved to see he was uninjured.

"Joshua fell off the end of the dock and I jumped in to get him," Tess said, pulling at her wet shirt.

"Oh dear, did you trip?" I asked Joshua.

Joshua shrugged his shoulders and glanced away.

"I told him to be careful not to fall in, but no sooner did I say it when he bent over to take a closer look at the minnows swimming by, and over the edge of the dock he went, head first!" Tess explained.

"Are you okay, Joshua?" I asked, gently squeezing his shoulder.

He nodded and exclaimed, "I swallowed some water!"

I responded, "I hope you didn't swallow any minnows as well!" which made Joshua giggle. "Thank you for jumping in after him, Tess."

"No problem," she said. "The water wasn't over his head, but I thought he might panic, so I jumped in to get him."

While Tess and Joshua changed into dry clothes for the second time, Tydon and Mac joined us in the cottage, and we sat down to eat. We were famished! We enjoyed a supper of barbecued smokies, pork and beans, and pasta salad, followed by watermelon for dessert. Not much was said until our plates were empty.

We went to bed early, all of us exhausted from the excitement and heat of the day. Around two o'clock in the morning, though, I was awakened by Tess calling from the loft.

"Mom, I think Joshua threw up!"

Mac and I bounced out of bed to check on Joshua, who was sleeping on the pull-out couch in the living room. Sure enough, Joshua, the sheets, and the quilt were all covered in gooey liquid, but Joshua was still asleep. We woke him up so we could clean him up.

"Oh, that was a bad burp," he said as we sat him up.

Mac and I looked at each other with puzzled expressions, holding back our chuckles. His response was surprisingly funny. After changing his pyjamas, stripping the couch of the dirty bedding, and washing his face, we tucked him in to an oversized down-filled sleeping bag. We figured Joshua might have felt sick from the heat and too much watermelon. But, though Joshua fell back asleep quickly, it took Mac and me a bit longer.

———————

The next morning, Joshua awoke early. I opened my eyes to his two big dark eyes peering at me as he stood still beside my bed, waiting for me to wake up. I decided it was best to get out of bed and make him a continental breakfast that he could eat quietly at the table. I turned the television on softly to watch one of my favourite Christian motivational speakers while Joshua gobbled down a carrot muffin and drank a big glass of milk without a word. While Joshua was eating, I left the room to put on shorts and a t-shirt. Upon returning, I noticed that Joshua was watching the television intently. My program had ended and another had started. The commentator was describing a poverty-stricken land, with scenes of destruction. I quickly turned the television off. Joshua set down his milk glass with a thud. The milk moustache above his lip made me smile.

"Would you like more milk?" I asked,

"No thank you. Can I go play in the sandbox?" he asked sweetly.

"Sure," I answered back.

I opened the side door and Joshua ran to the sandbox. The air was refreshing, and the peaceful sounds of nature in the early morning were worth the very early wake-up. The woodpecker, tapping away ever so diligently in the distance, the happy tweets of common prairie birds, and the familiar call of the two-note song of the male Black-capped Chickadee greeted us as we stepped outside. Soon those soothing nature songs would be muffled by the sound of boats zipping along on the water.

As I swept the deck off of bugs and the odd cobweb, another sound caught my attention. It was Joshua's voice booming loudly from the sandbox. I stopped to listen to his play-words.

"Now all the people were praying for someone to come and help them!"

I peered over at Joshua from the corner of the deck and noticed that he had set up the wood blocks into house-like structures. He then pushed a large toy tug boat smack into the middle of the houses, sending the blocks flying in all directions. My mind quickly recalled the program airing earlier this morning: a charity raising money for a devastated community, showing in detail the suffering, as well as people praying.

Joshua continued, "They don't have any food or anywhere to live."

Wow, he was bang on! I watched him in awe as he reiterated the events of the program. I stood silent, unsure if I should interrupt his play. One thing for sure, Joshua was like a sponge, soaking up everything from television programs to falling-off-the-dock experiences.

The back door opened, taking my attention away from Joshua. Tess, Tydon, and Mac brought out a tray of muffins and a carafe of coffee. Joshua came running over to us, tripping on the steps up to the deck and tumbling onto his belly.

He quickly got up and stated, "I'm okay!" He gave Tess a quick hug and asked me if he could have another muffin.

We all were enjoying the serene morning, sipping coffee, and chatting. Joshua began pulling on Mac's arm, asking if he would give him some pushes on the swing.

"Okay, little mister, let's give it a go!"

Suddenly, the morning serenity ended when sobs bellowed from the swing set. Joshua approached the deck holding his arms in the air, his elbows scratched and slightly bleeding. I took him inside, cleaned up the scratches, and put a *Paw Patrol* bandage on each one.

"What happened?" I asked Mac as we came back outside and Joshua ran to the sandbox.

"I was explaining to Joshua how to pull back on the ropes of the swing in order to move it, but he complained it was too hard. I gave him a couple of pushes to move things along. Then, as he was gaining a little bit of height, he just let go of the ropes! Off he flew, forward onto the grass," Mac replied in a defensive voice.

I could easily visualize how this happened. Mac and I were learning that Joshua needed continuous, consistent, positive, and patient guidance with everyday common activities. He didn't quite understand how his actions might have consequences, either good or bad, and tended to give up when a task became too hard. It took a lot of energy to teach him how to overcome challenging situations.

Mac, Joshua, and Tydon soon headed down to the dock. Joshua was interested in trying out his new fishing rod, unaware that it wouldn't actually hook a real live fish. After lunch, Tess and Tydon took the boat out for a cruise down the lake, but Joshua kept fishing with his new rod, even though the only thing he caught was sea weed.

Before long, the weekend had come to a close. Mac and I waved from the driveway as Tess and Tydon drove away. We waved until we couldn't see the car anymore, and I felt tears prickling at the corners of my eyes.

"Why are you crying?" Joshua asked, looking up at me.

"I'm crying because I love and miss Tess and Ty," I said.

He looked puzzled, but I didn't want to compare my situation to how he felt about Nanny and Pops.

Soon, we were on the road, back to the city and our chaotic lives.

CHAPTER EIGHT
A New Friend

WE AWOKE EARLY Monday morning, as I had a to-do list that needed attention. Mac was up early and headed out the front door to go to work.

Joshua jumped up from the table, just about knocking his cereal bowl off the table, and ran towards Mac. "Why do you always have to go to work?" He grabbed Mac's legs and squeezed tightly.

Mac responded, "I have to earn money to pay for the things we need like food and clothes." Mac peeled Joshua's arms away and gave him a fist bump, saying, "See you later!"

Joshua looked at me and asked, "What are we going to do today?"

"We are going to the grocery store to buy some food."

I fell deep into thought, remembering one of the more amusing visits Tess and I had the grocery store. I was paying for the items at the check-out station, and Tess was quietly sitting at the front of the cart. I handed over what must have seemed like a lot of money to the cashier, who took it with a happy "Thank you!" As we made our way out of the store, Tess blurted out, "When I grow up, I'm going to be a money taker!" I laughed at her odd but funny words, realizing that she had just observed me giving the cashier a lot of money, and she appeared to be just standing there accepting money.

I smiled at Tess and said, "Okay!"

And, wouldn't you know it? When Tess was sixteen years old, she worked part-time as a cashier at the same grocery store!

Joshua nudged my leg, noticing my silence. "Sara?"

I looked at him, "Yes, Joshua?"

"What's the matter?"

"Nothing, I was just thinking about going to the grocery store," I told him.

"Oh, can we buy Bear Paws?"

"Sure, you can help me do the shopping," I responded, smiling.

After our grocery trip, unloading and putting the groceries away, and eating lunch, Joshua went downstairs to play with dinosaurs and a medieval castle set. I heard growling noises rising from the basement and decided to take a peek at his noisy play. Joshua lined the dinosaurs up across the coffee table and couch, surrounding the castle, where the knights were positioned. Joshua attacked the knights with dinosaurs in both hands, squealing and growling while knocking over the knights with the dinosaurs! I started to laugh, startling Joshua.

He jumped up and yelled, "Sara, what are you doing there? You scared me!"

"I'm sorry, Joshua, I was watching you play."

"Why?" he asked, tilting his head to the side.

"I heard scary noises and I wanted to make sure you were okay," I said.

"Oh, I'm okay," he answered.

"Good to know, I hope the knights recover from the dinosaur attacks!" I laughed.

Joshua scrunched his face up and said, "The dinosaurs are eating them for lunch!"

"Oh dear!" I said. I left Joshua playing and went upstairs to fold laundry.

That night, after supper, Mac and Joshua headed outside. Joshua rode his bike around the bay while Mac cut the grass. It was then that the little girl who lived next door came outside. She noticed Joshua and slowly approached the sidewalk to get a better look at him. Mac noticed her curious demeanour.

"Hi, Jasmine!" he greeted her cheerfully.

"Who's that little boy?" she asked, pointing at Joshua.

"His name is Joshua. He'll be living with our family for a while."

Jasmine, a very inquisitive and bright girl of eight years old, loved to chat. Her response was careful and thoughtful. "When did he start living with you?"

"About two weeks ago," Mac said, walking towards Jasmine.

"Oh, I was away at Valley View Camp. It was awesome! We got to go horseback riding, hiking, swimming, and kayaking!"

Joshua rode up and Jasmine immediately greeted him with a happy, "Hi!"

Joshua looked up at Mac and then back at Jasmine. "Hi," he said shyly.

Without introducing herself, Jasmine asked Joshua if he wanted to draw with sidewalk chalk. He eagerly got of off his bike and joined Jasmine.

"Joshua, you need to take off your helmet and put your bike into the garage before you play with Jasmine," Mac said.

Joshua nodded and quickly put away his bike and helmet. Then he joined Jasmine on her driveway and they started colouring away with their sidewalk chalk.

Moments later, Glen and Diane, Jasmine's parents, came out to say hello. Joshua, who was bent over drawing with a purple piece of chalk, jumped up when he saw them and hid behind Mac's legs. He peeked out from behind Mac's knees, to get a better look at the neighbours. They warmly smiled at Joshua, greeting him with a compliment and encouragement.

"We saw you riding your bike around the island. You're really good at pushing your bike with your feet!" Diane said.

"You're fast too!" Glen added.

Jasmine asked Joshua if he wanted to ride bikes with her, and Mac allowed him to go. The kids grabbed their bikes and helmets, and off they both went, Joshua very proud that someone had noticed him doing something he was successful at.

After a brief visit with the neighbours, Mac turned off the underground sprinklers and tidied up the garage. Twenty minutes later, he called and waved at Joshua, who was now climbing the small structure with Jasmine located at the park entrance.

"It's time to come in!" Mac said.

Jasmine immediately listened to the request, but Joshua however needed a bit of coaxing. He made his way back to the bay just as I came outside, and the frown on his face told me he didn't want to come in yet. But, when I asked Jasmine if she would like to join me and Joshua on our morning walk with Piper the next day, he brightened. Both of them joyfully skipped over to Jasmine's house, Joshua waiting patiently outside of the house for Jasmine to return with a response after asking her parents' permission to join us. Thankfully, it was yes! We said goodnight, Joshua put his bike in the garage, and we all went inside.

Before calling it a night, I called to my longtime friend Marcy who had looked after our children when they were younger. I was praying that she was still in the childcare business. It had been a while since we needed childcare, but we needed somewhere for Joshua to go while I was teaching.

Marcy was great with kids, and she ran a great daycare. She was organized and planned out her days. She frequently baked homemade bread and cookies, and provided her children with nutritious meals. Most importantly, she loved her daycare kids as if they were her own.

So, imagine my relief when she said she had a spot open in her daycare. We arranged to meet the next afternoon so she could get to know Joshua and decide if she would take him into her daycare.

The next day, during lunch, I spoke with Joshua about the change in our afternoon routine. Usually, Joshua would have an hour of unstructured play followed by an hour of Treehouse television, but today we would go for a short afternoon walk to a family friend's house to say hello. Joshua thought this was great, as long as he could play

Hot Wheels when we returned home. So, we leashed up Piper and walked the fifteen minutes over to Marcy's house. In no time at all, we had reached the front steps of Marcy's home. I knocked, and Marcy opened the door.

"Well, hello!" she said warmly. "Who is this fine young man hiding behind you?"

I hadn't noticed that Joshua had quietly slipped behind me and stood frozen like a statue. I replied, "This is Joshua, he is staying with us for a while."

"Would Joshua like to come inside with you and have a freezie?" Marcy said with a smile.

Joshua smiled and nodded. He slipped around me and walked into Marcy's house. Marcy and I sat at the dining room table catching up, Piper curled up on the front entrance carpet for a snooze, and Joshua slurped his icy cool treat. Joshua seemed to capture Marcy's heart, just as he had caught mine the first time I met him at the park. Marcy asked Joshua a few questions regarding his favourite activities, to which he responded casually with two- to three-word answers. We had a pleasant visit, and I was confident she would take him into her daycare.

One hour later, we were walking out of the front door and headed home. En route to our house, we ran into more good friends of ours, Laura and Blake Wilson. They were packing up their truck to spend some time at their cottage, which happened to be located at the same lake as ours, just a different resort. We often visited them and sat around the campfire enjoying friendship and good food. We had also asked them to be character references for this foster placement. But, because everything happened so fast, I hadn't had the chance to tell them that Joshua was placed with us. It had only been a little under three weeks, but it felt like a lot longer.

As I introduced Joshua to Laura and Blake, once again, he instinctively hid behind me.

"You, Mac, and Joshua should come by our cottage Saturday night. We can watch the football game and Blake will do up some munchies on his new camping deep fryer," suggested Laura.

As soon as the word "munchies" came out of Laura's mouth, Joshua came out from behind me and curiously pondered these two new faces. Laura asked Joshua if he liked chicken fingers, and it was like she became his new best friend. He piped up with a loud "Yes!" and jumped up and down. And so, we decided to gather at the Wilson's cottage at next Saturday night.

CHAPTER NINE

Beach Break

MAC AND I loaded up the truck for a three-week stay at the cottage. We were both looking forward to a longer stint of time to enjoy the rest and relaxation that came with beach life. We arrived mid-afternoon, giving us plenty of time to go for a short walk along a winding path through the hills behind our cottage. The humid air made us feel like camels carrying heavy loads.

As soon as we returned to the cottage, Joshua splashed around in the inflatable pool I had purchased a couple of days previously. Mac placed the pool at the bottom of the big yellow slide and filled it to the brim. Joshua was up and down the stairs for over an hour while Mac and I clapped for him from the deck where we were relaxing. He yelled out from the top of the slide, "Watch me!"

By nine that evening, we were all sapped out!

I awoke the next morning to a little face staring at me. It was very early. My brain moved slowly as I tried to think of how to explain the concept of "sleeping in" to Joshua.

"Go back to bed," was all I could come up with.

He chirped, "It's morning, time to get up!"

In July, the sun rises around five o'clock in the morning. Our cottage faced the east, and the wall of windows filled our abode with bright sunshine every morning.

"How about you go play cars quietly?" I said sleepily.

Then I immediately realized my mistake. Car noises are not quiet! But, Joshua eagerly ran off, content that he didn't have to go back to bed, and soon the sounds of car motors reverberated from the living room. I decided to get up and let Mac sleep in.

As I walked into the kitchen, Joshua greeted me happily. I tried to respond the same, but my eyes were still small slits and my body lethargically moved toward the coffee pot. Joshua gave me a big hug and then returned to his car pile. I glanced at the clock on the stove: six o'clock. I knew I'd have to take an afternoon nap, or our visit to the Wilson's cottage may be shorter than planned. I plunked myself onto the couch with my cup of coffee.

Joshua jumped up, threw his hands up in the air, and asked, "What are we going to do today?"

I looked out at the lake; it was like glass. "We can go kayaking. The water is nice and calm, perfect for a paddle down the lake!"

"What's kayaking?" Joshua asked.

"A kayak is like a canoe, but you sit on your butt instead of your knees, and the paddle is different too," I said, taking a sip of coffee.

"What's a canoe?" Joshua tilted his head to the side.

"It's a long small boat without a motor." I pointed to a photo on the wall behind Joshua of Mac and me, each of us sitting inside a blue kayak on the water, taken last summer.

Joshua looked at the photo and then back at me with uncertainty. I reassured him that we could tie the kayak up to the dock and he could float safely and securely not far from the shore.

With that, I got up and made us both some breakfast.

Mac and I carried the kayaks down to the dock. Joshua watched as we slowly navigated our way down to the dock. I was eager to go for a kayak ride before the speed boats made large rolling waves that rocked small vessels to the point of an uncomfortable ride. Joshua watched as I boarded my kayak, carefully sitting in the small space carved out of the long banana shaped boat. I paddled out and away from the dock, then back again to reassure Joshua that this activity was safe and quite enjoyable. Mac jumped into the water for a quick swim to cool off, and Joshua sat on the edge of the dock with his feet in the water. Mac encouraged Joshua to get into the water. It took a bit, but finally Mac held Joshua in his arms and carried him in the water close to the dock. Joshua squeezed Mac's neck tightly. Mac tried to explain that the life jacket Joshua was wearing would keep his head above water and help him float.

I knew that Jan often took Joshua swimming at the indoor pool in their neighbourhood and attended a swim class designed to help children relax and gain confidence in the water, but she also mentioned that he was afraid and it took quite a while for him to become comfortable in the water.

However, secure in Mac's embrace, Joshua became comfortable enough in the water to let go. He began to float in front of Mac, and a smile spread across his face. A new confidence was taking hold.

"Is it hard to kayak?" he called to me from the water.

"No, it's not hard, but you need to sit very still and balance when you are in a kayak," I said, paddling closer. "Would you like to try to maybe just sit in the kayak? Mac will tie your kayak to the dock and you don't have to paddle anywhere."

After a moment of thought, Joshua agreed. Mac tied the front of the kayak to one of the dock posts and lifted Joshua into it. Joshua's hands gripped the side of the kayak as it shook, but Mac stood right beside him, assuring Joshua that he would not leave his side. Once Joshua felt comfortable sitting in the kayak, Mac pulled it around and about the front of the dock. Then he sat on the edge of the dock, pushing it out and pulling it in with the attached rope. Joshua giggled and cheered as he enjoyed this easy and affixed boat glide. Finally, Mac gave Joshua the paddle to try moving the kayak on his own while still anchored to the dock. Joshua awkwardly dipped his paddle into the water. He wasn't able to move much, but he was happy with his progress, and he called out to me.

"Look, Sara, I'm kayaking!"

"Way to go!" I cheered.

He smiled from ear to ear. After a while the wind picked up making it challenging to float and boat, and we decided to head back up to the cottage. I quickly snapped a couple of photos of Joshua sitting in the kayak before Mac helped him out.

Around four-thirty, we changed clothes and packed a travel cooler full of snacks for Joshua, as well as bottles of cold water, ice tea and pop. I also packed a back pack of warmer clothes for evening wear, and we headed out to the Wilson's. We first drove through our resort of Copper Valley, then through the resort of Sunny Lake, and finally into the resort of Sand Hills, to the Wilson's lodge, a quaint summer home tucked away in rolling hills and thick vegetation.

They greeted us with waves and smiles. We gathered on the Wilson's outdoor covered deck, where a large screen television on the wall showed the beginnings of the football game.

As the football game proceeded, so did the evening. Joshua received a lot of attention. He didn't seem to be as shy as usual, perhaps because he kept himself busy by munching down all of the delicious appetizers that Blake cooked in his new campfire deep fryer: wings, ribs, chicken fingers, onion rings, jalapeño cheese poppers—the perfect cuisine for football, friends, and, of course, one little boy.

"These chicken fingers are so good!" Joshua said. "I could move in with you and eat these every day, but then you would have to do my laundry!"

Laura chuckled. "Maybe you can visit again and we'll make sure to fry up some chicken fingers for you!"

This sounded good to Joshua, he walked over and gave Laura a long hug. Joshua then explored the cottage grounds. He carefully crossed over the ravine by walking over a wooden bridge, which led to a hiking trail around the outskirts of the property. The entire loop was a five-minute walk, and it brought him right back to where he started. Joshua enjoyed following the trail for quite some time, spotting all sorts of little critters. We could hear his squeals of surprise and delight when a gopher or rabbit crossed his path. After a while, he tired out and snuggled up beside Laura.

We bid our adieus once the football game was over and climbed into the truck for the dark ride home. The road didn't have street lights, but the patio lights shining from the cottages we passed helped light the road. Joshua fell asleep two minutes into the ride back to our cottage. Thirty minutes later, Mac carried Joshua into the cottage, and I helped a drowsy little boy change into his pyjamas and then tucked him into bed.

Regardless of how late Joshua went to sleep at night, he always awoke very early. I always told him that he was "up with the chickens," who started their day at the break of dawn as well.

Mac planned to work on extending our cottage deck, which wrapped around two sides of the cottage, throughout the day. Mac would be building the frame of the deck for the north side of the cottage.

As Mac started setting out his tools, Joshua asked if he could help with the project. Mac and I thought this would be a useful way to help Joshua develop his fine motor skills and learn a bit about construction work, so Mac dug out our oldest child's youth tool belt from the garage for Joshua to wear and slipped a few tools into the pockets. He gave Joshua a hard hat for his head, tightening it up around Joshua's chin, and instantly Joshua was ready to take on the job of a deck craftsman. Plus, he looked super cute!

Joshua proved to be a good helper: holding the tape measure for Mac or handing Mac his pencil and other tools when he needed them. When Joshua noticed that Mac wore his pencil behind his ear, Joshua asked for a pencil of his own. I gave him one, and Joshua immediately stuck it behind his ear, a cheeky grin appeared on his face. He went back to Mac, who smiled upon seeing where Joshua had put his pencil.

The rest of the morning passed the same way, with Joshua helping Mac with small tasks. After a while, when Mac needed to concentrate on a bigger task, he set Joshua up with a small hammer and a board that had nails pounded into it about a quarter of an inch deep. Joshua kept himself busy pounding the nails deeper into the board for over an hour. He was very proud of his personal building project.

Later in the day, towering cumulonimbus clouds began to form, and the bright blue sky began to deepen into a mix of dark grey and blue. Soon, light rain showers developed into a downpour. The abrupt change in weather didn't seem to faze Joshua at first. He seemed oblivious to the possible storm brewing ahead. We stood quietly looking out of the front windows as the pelting rain formed fast-flowing rivers along the stone pathway beside the cottage. Suddenly, the wind picked up and knocked a lawn chair off of the deck. Joshua pressed his nose against the window with curiosity to see where the chair landed.

Then, at the first booming sound of thunder and sharp lightning flash, he grabbed Mac's hand and said, "It sounds like the sky is crashing down!"

Mac looked at Joshua, who was now covering his eyes with his hands. Mac immediately picked up Joshua in his arms to comfort him. I scooted up the stairs to the upper-level of the loft to get a better view of the living sky and fullness of the first summer storm.

Mac sat Joshua down on the couch and then settled himself beside Joshua. I returned to the main level, put *The Land Before Time* movie into the VCR, and sat down on the other side of Joshua. Ten minutes into the movie the power went off, casting the inside of the cottage into pitch darkness.

"Uh-oh," said Joshua.

"No worries," Mac responded quickly. Mac got up and went down the hallway to grab a flashlight from the storage closet. Joshua tucked his head into my side while waiting for Mac to return. Moments later, Mac was back, flashing the light across the wall.

Joshua lifted his head and said, "Can I try?"

For the next hour, he was preoccupied with the flashlight and forgot all about the storm. He even went to sleep with the flashlight.

The rest of our time at the cottage passed quickly. We spent our days at the dock or playing in the yard. One afternoon, Mac and Joshua carried child-sized lawn furniture up to the top level of the tree house. Up and down Joshua went, furnishing his "house," as he called it, with pails, toys, and other items that he could scrounge up to decorate his place. This became his favourite place to spend time during our stay at the cottage. He often ate his lunch in up in the tree house. He also concocted pretend meals of berries, twigs, and leaves from the bushes, and he carried up pails of minnows he had caught in his fishing net. We were never quite sure of their purpose, but it was his house!

No quicker than we arrived, we were packing up to go back home. We had thoroughly enjoyed our vacation at the cabin, and planned to come back on weekends during August. And good thing, too: we didn't know it yet, but the storms and challenges of life were about to break forth.

CHAPTER TEN
A Trip to the Big City

MAC RETURNED TO work, while Joshua and I returned to our routine. In four short days, we would be on our way to Barrington to celebrate Mac's father's eightieth birthday. Barrington was in another county and took approximately seven hours to drive to, including two stops to stretch legs, have a snack and walk the dog. We booked a hotel for our two-night stay, thinking this would be easier since we were now toting an active four-year-old and his essential gear.

Two days before we planned to leave, we had a scheduled visit with Cassy, Joshua's case worker. When we mentioned our trip plans, she asked if we had secured permission to take Joshua out of the county, and I realized my oversight; I hadn't completed the form. My heart sank. The only other option was for Joshua and me to stay behind, and Mac would go alone to his father's birthday dinner and party. But Cassy graciously said she would do her best of fill out the forms and, thankfully, a letter was approved for Joshua.

The long drive went a lot smoother than we thought. Joshua actually slept for most of it! We made our first stop at a rest area just a couple miles off the highway after two-and-a-half hours for a breath of fresh air, enjoying a picnic lunch and walking Piper around the grounds.

During the second part of our trip, Joshua peppered us with questions.

"How many more miles?"

"Are we there yet?"

"I'm bored. I'm hungry."

We had made many trips to Barrington over the years, and we were well prepared for these common gripes. I gave Joshua a Ziploc bag filled with Cheerios, raisins, and pretzels and popped in his favourite DVD. Before long, Joshua was happy, laughing, and fairly content.

The last two hours of the drive were a little more trying. We played "I Spy," sang funny songs, looked at picture books, and worked on pencil and paper activities until Joshua nodded off again. We decided to keep driving, rather than make a second stop for a break. Joshua awoke just as we were approaching the outskirts of Barrington. He peered out of the window, gazing at the outline of the city buildings ahead.

"Look at all the tall buildings!" he said excitedly. "How come there are so many cars? Where are we going?"

"We're going to stay in a hotel," I said, glancing back at him.

"What's a hotel?"

"A hotel is a big building with many rooms. The rooms have beds and a bathroom, and people can pay money to live in the room if they're far away from home and need a place to stay."

Once we were settled in our room on the main floor, Joshua and I took Piper for a walk. We made our way through the hotel parking lot to the back of the property, following a path alongside the river that flowed through Barrington. We walked for about fifteen minutes before returning to the hotel room. As we passed the indoor pool and water slide on our way back, Joshua caught sight of the children screaming and laughing as they shot like rockets down the slide, on their bellies, on their butts. I asked him if he would like to check out the pool during our stay, but he just looked at me and shrugged his shoulders. Soon, we set off again to make the forty-five-minute drive to Mac's parents' house.

It was wonderful to see Mac's parents, Elsa and Josef, his brother, and his brother's family again. After hugs and greetings, we sat down to the delicious meal Elsa insisted on making, even though she was eighty-one.

Joshua keenly watched each family member as we heaped large portions of foods onto our plate.

"What's that?" he asked curiously, pointing to a serving dish in the middle of the table.

"Strudel," Elsa replied. "Have you ever eaten strudel before?" Joshua shrugged his shoulders, and Mac gave him a small piece of strudel to try.

Joshua chewed his bite thoughtfully. "Yum! Can I have some too?"

Mac dished up strudel, schnitzel, a type of meat, and spaetzle noodles onto Joshua's plate. Joshua devoured every morsel!

After supper, Mac offered to help his mom with the dishes. She stubbornly refused; it was a battle of the wills. Eventually, those of us at the dinner table tried to distract her with conversation, and Mac slipped in and out of the kitchen to do what he could without his mom intervening, she did however call out several times, "Mac, just leave it, I will clean up tomorrow!"

By ten o'clock, we all shuffled out of the front door, tired, happy, and our bellies full.

_____

The next day, we dressed ourselves up in our Sunday best and headed to a restaurant for the second birthday dinner. We sat at a long rectangular table for twelve, where Mac's sister-in-law had decorated the chairs with large colourful balloons. A flower centrepiece furnished the table, adding cheer to our festivities. After dinner, we gathered back at Elsa and Josef's house for birthday cake and coffee, enjoying a family visit.

While the adults talked, Joshua explored every nook and cranny in Mac's parents' house with Elsa and bombarded her with questions.

"What's this?"

"Whose room is this?"

"Where are your kids?"

Though he didn't seem to understand that Mac was her oldest son, nonetheless "Mama," as we fondly called her, answered all of Joshua's questions in detail. Elsa was quite taken with Joshua, and he was absolutely fond of her.

Finally, after many endearing hugs and promises to see each other soon, we returned to our hotel. It was near eleven in the evening by the time we got back, and Piper frantically greeted us at the door, needing a short walk. Mac grabbed her leash to take her while I helped Joshua brush his teeth before tucking him in to bed. He groggily asked for a bedtime story, and I agreed, knowing he would fall asleep before the story ended. Sure enough, he fell asleep after the first two pages.

We all awoke to the sound of Piper barking and bouncing by the door of our hotel room. She desperately needed to go outside! Mac quickly dressed and escorted piper down the hallway to the outside entrance of the hotel. Joshua sat up in bed and piped up, "Sara, what can we do?" I responded, "Let's go for a quick dip in the swimming pool!" Joshua tilted his eyebrows and unenthusiastically replied with a simple "Ok". Joshua and I sat at the edge of the pool dangling our feet into the cool water. Joshua was not interested in swimming, so he sat quietly watching me as I completed a couple of laps, then I decided to check out the water slide. I was surprised at the speed the water moved me down the slide! The force pushed me quickly into a final awkward tumble and drop, creating a loud splash into the pool! I swam over to Joshua and asked if he would like to ride down the water slide with me. Joshua shook his head, got up, an walked toward the hot tub. I followed him and we both enjoyed a warm soak!

We left for Rockport shortly after breakfast, and Joshua slept most of the drive home. He was so overtired that the humming of the truck rocked him back to sleep every time he opened his eyes. This short whirlwind trip, filled with non-stop activities, was tiring for all of us.

CHAPTER ELEVEN
Reality Check

THE END OF summer was near. The cooler summer evenings signalled that it was time to return to my classroom and prepare it for my new students. I spent the last two weeks in August organizing my classroom for the months ahead.

As I was preparing for the work my classroom needed, Mac and I received a call from social services. They told us that we needed to schedule visits with Cassy every two weeks, as well as visits with Rachael, the social worker assigned to us as Joshua's foster parents. We were surprised that we required a worker, but social services explained that if we needed representation in any circumstance, she would handle it, just as Cassy handled issues pertaining to Joshua. We agreed that the best time of day to meet for all of us would be consistently at four-thirty in the afternoon, and we scheduled the first two visits back-to-back the following Thursday.

――――――――――

Joshua was eager to help me with the enormous task of setting up my brand-new classroom. The first few days were consumed with transporting my "teacher stuff" to the school. Then, we spent the morning and afternoon organizing my classroom. He helped me with everything I asked him to do. He sorted toys for various centres, he posted pictures on the bulletin board, and played! This was the kindergarten classroom, after all, a four-year-old boy's dream. There were no shortage of activities to keep him busy. Before long, car noises were coming out of his mouth, I looked over to where he was stationed, lo and behold he had found the transportation centre!

At five-fifteen Mac showed up as planned. Mac helped move and arrange the heavy furniture and plugged in some of the technological equipment, which had been disconnected during the painting process, ensuring that it was working. It can be said that only a teacher's loving and supportive spouse knows what goes on behind the scenes in the day and life of an educator. I was so thankful for this extra set of helping hands.

———————

Leaves were beginning to fall from some of the trees along the road to our cottage. Periodically, deer would sprint across our way, surprising Joshua, before disappearing into the rolling hills. Many animals shared the prairie resort with us: coyotes, squirrels, gophers, raccoons, beavers, moose, red foxes, a wide variety of birds, snakes, frogs, and of course mice. We always enjoyed seeing most of these amazing critters and crawlers.

Our weekend was consumed with enjoying one last ride on the personal watercraft and the boat. Joshua and Mac ripped around on the larger three-seater jet ski, Joshua sitting in front of Mac and holding on to the handle bars, and Mac sitting behind him, reaching around to steer. I rode the smaller two-seater jet ski, zipping around the lake enjoying every moment of the ride. Mac took it a little slower, as Joshua was just beginning to feel comfortable joy-riding on the open water.

Eventually, we hauled the jet skis out of the water and back to our cottage to store in the garage for the winter. Next, we went for one last boat ride. We sped up and down the lake, a two-hour cruise, with a couple of stops to jump off the back of the boat's platform to cool off with a refreshing swim. Joshua had developed confidence over the summer, and he slowly and carefully jumped out to Mac or me, our arms open to catch him.

Finally, I dropped Mac off at our dock. He changed into dry clothes and drove the truck and trailer down to the public boat launch. Joshua stayed with me in the boat, and we puttered our way down the lake to meet Mac at the public dock. As soon as he saw us, he backed the trailer into the water. I guided the boat toward the dock and before long the boat was securely fastened to the trailer and we were on our way back to the cottage. Joshua and I sat in the boat as Mac cautiously hauled us back to the cottage. The ride was bumpy and tree branches often grazed our heads. At times we ducked to avoid being whipped in the face by the odd branch extending over the road. Joshua seemed to find this dry-land travel quite exciting; he laughed and giggled the entire drive back. Although I enjoyed this experience with Joshua, melancholy feelings overwhelmed me. It would be another nine long months before we would have the pleasure of leisurely gallivanting on the lake in our boat on a warm summer day.

Once back at the cottage, we barbecued supper: steak and potatoes, garlic bread, and corn on the cob. The afternoon's seasonal chores of removing the boat and sea-doos from the water, as well as a final joy ride on each, tuckered all three of us out, and we devoured our meal. We sat on the front deck after supper, looking out upon the lake, watching as families sped along in their boats and enjoying the remainder of what summer offered. Tomorrow would bring another day of end of season cottage jobs that needed to be tackled before we could go home.

CHAPTER TWELVE
Back to Routine

I COULD FEEL my stomach twist and turn Sunday around supper time, but not because I was hungry—my nerves were a little on edge. Tomorrow was my first day of work at my new school. County teachers returned to work during the final week of August, which consisted of meetings and professional development, classroom organization, and program development. Students would not be in attendance until next week, however, new colleagues, a new school, and new procedures and protocols had me feeling anxious. Mac had taken this week off from work to care for Joshua, as our formal child care would not begin until after the September long weekend. The weather forecast was above average temperatures so Mac, Joshua, and Piper planned to return to the cottage later today for the first half of the week.

Sleep could not find me. I had not tossed and turned, or struggled to sleep, since June when it seemed everything I knew and was comfortable with was changing. Once again, my world was uncertain. Deep in my heart, I knew this career move was the divine plan of God. This change was good. After all, I had made the choice to seek out employment that was in line with biblical traditional family values and truth.

I fell asleep with that thought and awoke to a quiet house, around five-thirty in the morning. I was hoping to add my early morning run and devotional reading to my day. These two basic activities I relied on to remove stress and anxiety, and bring peace, which had taken a back seat over the summer holidays. At five-forty-five, I made my way out of the house in my running gear and went for a thirty-minute walk-run.

Upon returning home, I was startled when I opened the door: there stood Joshua, waiting for me.

"Why did you run away?" he asked.

I shook my head and bent down to Joshua's level. "I didn't run away; I went for a run to get some exercise," I said. "Can you go back to sleep until Mac wakes up?"

"But I'm not tired anymore!"

"How about you look at some books in your room until Mac gets up? I need to do a few things before I go to work today," I said softly.

"Why do you have to go to work?"

This question was familiar, and I knew my answer wouldn't suffice, so I gave Joshua a choice: "You can go and look at books, or you can go back to sleep."

Joshua scurried off to his room, as fast as his little legs could go. Moments later I heard him making up words to the pictures in the books he was looking at, a strategy I had been teaching him over the past few weeks to build his interest in reading.

I made my way to the kitchen, where I poured myself a hot cup of coffee with a bit of cream and sat down at the kitchen island to read my Bible and the devotion for the given date.

Before long, I was on my way to school. The day passed very quickly. By four o'clock, I was spent. I decided to make the most of my time without Mac and Joshua. I grabbed a snack out of my lunch bag and began to work on next weeks lesson plans. At seven in the evening, I went home, tired but confident that all was good thus far. I recounted the many new faces and names I had encountered through-out the day during my drive home, encouraging, helpful voices, asking if I needed anything and welcoming me.

———————

The day of our visits with the social workers arrived. Both came to our house on Thursday at four-thirty. Joshua was riding his bike around the bay, and it wasn't easy to get him to come inside the house to chat with Cassy until we suggested he challenge her to an air hockey game. Mac and I talked with Rachael while Joshua and Cassy played a few rounds on the air hockey table in the basement. Joshua then gave Cassy a tour of the house, including showing her the contents of every single drawer in his bedroom. He was very proud of his room and everything it contained.

After that, we sat down at the kitchen table for a group chat. We were surprised to find out that Joshua's family visits were re-starting in September, with the first one scheduled for Saturday afternoon. Joshua paid little to no attention to this part of the conversation. He had vague memories of his biological family as most of his first four years were spent with Steve and Jan. He periodically went to live with his biological parents, only to return to the Taylors after unsuccessful attempts to reunite the family for reasons not disclosed to Mac and me. When we first started fostering Joshua, we were informed that family visits were not in the near future, if at all.

Once both social workers had left, Mac and I talked a bit about this new development. The short notice, along with our uncertainty and lack of information, left us feeling bewildered and confused. We decided to take it one day at a time.

CHAPTER THIRTEEN

change of season, change in Groove

SEPTEMBER WAS UPON us in full throttle. We made one last overnight trip to the cottage to store seasonal items for the winter. Joshua played along the shoreline as Mac and I removed the dock from the water. We were hoping to make a day trip in October to rake the leaves and enjoy the ever-changing fall colours. Mac was on the road for work a lot, often arriving home later than usual, and I added childcare drop-off and pick-up to my daily routine, a long-forgotten chore that required me to make extra time in the morning and after school. School was going well, but I couldn't keep track of all the new procedures and protocols. Everyday introduced newness in some form or shape. One thing remained the same: kids are kids, no matter where a teacher is stationed!

Joshua was getting along well at daycare. He immediately took to Marcy. Her sense of humour and upbeat personality helped him to adjust without hesitation. He was also very fond of his new playmates! One little girl and two little boys, the exact same age as Joshua, as well as a toddler and a baby made up the crew of children under Marcy's care. A small group of sweet little people!

One night early in the week while I was reading Joshua a bedtime story, he looked away from the storybook and at my face with serious intention. "Sara, now that summer's done, am I going back to live with Nanny and Pops?" he said.

I put the book down and decided that it was probably a good time to redirect his attention. I thought it interesting that, after the fun-filled summer, his memories of Jan and Steve didn't fade and he continued to display deep affection for them. First, I told him that on Saturday, we were going to do something very special. Next, we prayed. We prayed for every single person Joshua and I could think of: Nanny and Pops, the little girl that lived next door to them, his biological siblings, and his parents.

———————

On Saturday morning, Joshua helped me bake cupcakes. Mac and I had decided not to tell Joshua about his visit with his family until Saturday morning so that he wouldn't have too much time to worry about it, as he hadn't seen his biological family in a year. I hoped that baking cupcakes would help Joshua feel at ease while I told him about the visit, and I planned for him to take the cupcakes for his family to enjoy.

As Joshua stirred the thick chocolate batter, I began to talk with him about his siblings. Joshua looked into the batter bowl as he continued to moved the wooden spoon around and around. I then brought up his mom and dad.

"Do you remember Miranda and Theodore?" I asked Joshua.

"No,' he responded, as he lifted the stirring spoon out of the batter, inspecting the chocolatey goo.

"How about Sean, Jake, Anna, or Alicia?" I asked.

Joshua looked at me puzzled and responded, "I think I remember those names."

"They are your brothers and sisters," I said.

Joshua did not say anything more about his siblings, instead he moved the conversation back to our baking project. "Can we make chocolate icing and put some sprinkles on top?"

"Yes, that's a great idea! These cupcakes will be very tasty and look so colourful. We should share them with others!" I responded enthusiastically.

"Can I eat one first?"

"Yes, you can be the taste tester."

Joshua smiled and picked out the sprinkles from my Lazy Susan shelf as I poured the batter into the cupcake pan and slid them into the oven.

The smell of the cupcakes baking had Mac joining us in the kitchen for breakfast, and he poured himself a bowl of cereal. As Mac and Joshua ate their cereal, Mac said, "You know, Joshua, today is an important day."

Joshua glanced up from his bowl.

"That's right," I said. "You'll be able to share your cupcakes with your brothers and sisters this afternoon."

Joshua didn't say anything at first. Then, he chose his words carefully. "Is it a visit?" I couldn't tell by his expression if he felt good about this news. I responded, "Yes, it is."

"Oh." Joshua put down his spoon. "Can I decorate the cupcakes now?"

"Soon. They'll need to cool down first, but you can make the icing with me."

Joshua enjoyed icing and decorating the cupcakes. As agreed, he chose one cupcake to taste, but he only licked the icing off of the top of the cupcake and set it down on the table after a couple bites.

"I'm not hungry," he mumbled, looking down at the table.

"I'll wrap it up and save it for later for you," I said, grabbing a container from the cupboard and setting the cupcake in it.

With that, Joshua got dressed in jeans, a t-shirt, and a sweater and brushed his teeth. We combed his hair, and I told him he looked very handsome.

"Can I watch Treehouse?" he asked.

"Of course, I'll turn on the television and pull out the Lego table and buckets for you to build with while you watch your favourite programs."

I heard a few giggles from Joshua as he watched his cartoons. I peeked on him without making myself known to make sure all was well. He did not seem to interested in the Lego, however, he was content. I quickly showered and dressed in my favourite jeans and sweater.

Later, Joshua picked at his lunch. He told me his tummy had butterflies in it. I understood.

"How about we stop at McDonald's after your visit and pick up a Happy Meal?" I suggested.

"Can I play at the indoor play land too?" he asked.

Though I was planning on ordering at the drive-through, I decided we could make time for that. "Sure!" I answered.

We packed up the cupcakes and left the house for the afternoon. Occasionally, during our car travels, we listened to a CD. We would usually sing at the top of our lungs, smiling and giggling at words in the song that were amusing to Joshua. But today, Joshua wasn't in a singing mood. He peered out of the car window, expressionless.

———————

We arrived fifteen minutes early. As we entered the concrete building that housed the Institute of Child Services, Joshua said, "I remember this place."

We walked through two sets of glass doors and checked in. I promised Joshua that I would wait for him in the public seating area provided for visitors, and a young lady escorted him down the hallway and through another set of doors. I sat down on a black metal chair and waited as the hour ticked by.

Soon, Joshua, two of his siblings, and his mom walked through the double doors at the end of the hallway. Joshua ran into my arms, giving me a tight hug.

"Hi, I'm Joshua's mom, Miranda. This is Jake and Sean. Joshua's dad and sisters couldn't be here today," said the woman, shaking my hand.

She appeared frail and haggard. Her long hair hung down her back and partially covered her tired face. However, her handshake grip was strong and solid.

"Hello," I said.

"I want to thank you for looking after Joshua. I miss him so much," Miranda said, dropping my hand. "He's my baby of the bunch. I don't know what is going on with my children, I've been away for awhile and my health isn't so good."

I nodded; my mind couldn't come up with the right comfort words at the moment. I really didn't expect to meet Joshua's mom today or engage in conversation.

"Thank you for the cupcakes, we really appreciated and enjoyed them. Joshua didn't want to eat one though," Miranda continued.

"You're welcome. Joshua helped bake them this morning and ate one before the visit today, he was probably full of cupcake and not too hungry," I said, though I knew in my heart that wasn't the case.

Miranda picked up Joshua and pulled him close, but Joshua pulled away. My heart broke to watch; Miranda was a stranger to him.

We said goodbye and headed back to our car. Joshua was very quiet. I turned the music off just in case he wanted to talk, but he didn't. Ten minutes later, I pulled into the McDonald's parking lot. As soon as Joshua saw the golden arches, he sat up tall and cheered. I smiled, happy that he appeared to be coming out of his sullen mood.

Inside, I ordered a Happy Meal for Joshua, and he chose a toy that came with it. After chowing down his cheeseburger and fries, and drinking his milk, Joshua ran to the indoor play place. I watched as he carefully slid down the slide and jumped in the ball pit. I also noticed he seemed to watch the other children wistfully, and I wondered what he was thinking. After he tired himself out, he made his way back to our table. We cleared away our empty food wrappers and left the restaurant.

As we walked to the car, thunder rolled in the distance.

Joshua looked up at the sky and commented, "It's getting dark outside, just like it did when it stormed at the cottage."

"Yes it is," I agreed with Joshua.

Like the day's weather, I also felt gloomy with uncertainty in my heart. My emotions after this first visit were mixed. I was glad that Joshua had a chance to visit with his mom and brothers, yet I was uncomfortable with the situation as well.

I decided to make a stop at the mall before returning home. I turned into the parking lot and found a spot to park near one of the entrances.

Joshua quickly asked, "Why are we stopping here?"

I responded emphatically, "You need a snowsuit for winter."

Joshua argued, "But it's not snowing!"

I nodded my head and helped him out of the car. I took his hand in mine and we hustled along quickly, hoping to beat the rain. Once inside, I replied to his comment, "I know how much you enjoy playing outside, so I want to get you a nice snowsuit before they are all picked over."

Joshua looked at me, tilted his head, and asked, "Picked over?"

I looked toward him, smiled, and said, "Hopefully we can find one that you like and fits you comfortably!"

During the drive home from the mall—new snowsuit folded neatly in a shopping bag—Joshua fell sound asleep in the car. Mac was in the garage and heard us pull onto the driveway. He immediately came out to greet us. Joshua awoke and sat quietly.

"How was the visit?" Mac asked cheerfully as he opened the car door.

I responded with concern, "It was solemn."

I didn't think this was the answer Mac was expecting, but I couldn't think of another word to describe the experience for myself or Joshua. Mac carried Joshua inside the house. After a bowl of chicken noodle soup, Joshua stumbled to his bedroom, mumbling, "I'm tired."

CHAPTER FOURTEEN
It's sunday

WE AWOKE BY seven Sunday morning and got ready for church. Joshua had many questions regarding "church" and "Sunday school," as he had never attended a worship service before. I answered his questions while I popped a roast into the slow cooker for supper.

"What's a church?"

I looked over at him from the counter, where I was preparing supper, and answered, "A church is a group of people that gather together to worship Jesus, pray, and thank God."

"Is Sunday school like a real school?"

"It's similar, you learn about God with kids who are the same age as you."

Joshua paused from eating his breakfast and rested his head in his hands. He began to ask a series of questions to my answers.

"Is it fun?"

"It's super fun! You sing songs, read stories from the Bible, colour, play games, and you even get a snack to eat!"

"What's a Bible?"

"A Bible is a book that God gave us to learn about him, how we should live, and learn about who Jesus is."

"Is it the same as my storybooks?"

"There are many wonderful stories in the Bible. How about I buy you your own children's Bible and we can read a story every night before bedtime?"

"Can I come with you to buy it?"

"Certainly!"

"When?"

"Next week, but right now you need to get dressed for church."

The two of us made our way to Joshua's room. He hopped all the way there, opened the closet door, and joyfully picked out his favourite clothing.

Upon arriving at church, we registered Joshua in Sunday school, then we made our way into the church sanctuary just as the worship team was getting started. We sat near the back where multiple rows of chairs were reserved for families with young children, which allowed them to slip out of the service after worship to attend Sunday school without too much disruption. Worship was lively, and Joshua was drawn in by the sounds of the guitars, keyboard, drums, wind instruments, and voices all singing and playing in perfect unison and harmony. Soon, the music stopped, and the pastor took centre stage. I led Joshua toward the preschoolers Sunday school room. He was somewhat shy of the adult volunteer, but, as soon as he saw other children, he ran off to join them. I slipped back to the service quickly and quietly.

Mac and I went to pick up Joshua after the service. Joshua proudly displayed a piece of art work that he had worked on during Sunday school and began to describe his picture. We were thankful he revealed this information, as we couldn't have guessed what he had drawn in a million years, and praised him for his work. After coffee and juice, we drove to the grocery store for our weekly shopping trip. Joshua sat in the front seat of the shopping cart. He barely fit, Mac heaved and hoed while lifting him up and into the small space the cart provided. The store always provided samples for taste testing. This kept Joshua munching away as we made our way up and down the aisles filling our cart with food items needed and on our list for the next two weeks.

All of a sudden, Joshua blurted out, "That man has a lot of groceries in his tummy!" as he pointed at an oncoming shopper.

Mac and I were speechless and embarrassed of Joshua's comments, and the man frowned at us. However, both Mac and I agreed that Joshua stated his opinion very uniquely. "Too many groceries in our tummies" became our catch phrase whenever we over-ate a delicious meal.

Before long, we were in the check-out line paying for our groceries and on our way home. Joshua was a very good helper, carrying the groceries from our vehicle into the house and placing items on the kitchen counter. After everything was stored away in the refrigerator or cupboards, we had a light lunch of grilled cheese sandwiches and pickles, and then I made a few sides to go with our supper, for which my dad, David, would be joining us.

My dad arrived around five-thirty. He was a quiet-natured man, who lived one day at a time. He dearly missed my mom, who had gone to be with the Lord a couple years previously. Joshua had met him over the summer when he stopped by the house one evening to say hello and enjoy a glass of sweet tea with us. Joshua took a liking to him very quickly. My dad spoke genuinely with Joshua about his areas of interest, and the two of them had the most unique conversations. As soon as my dad arrived, Joshua flew to the door to show him the picture he created in Sunday school.

Dinner passed well, but not without incident. While passing the gravy to my dad, I accidentally knocked over his glass and spilled juice all over his shirt. I was horrified and rushed to give my dad a tea towel to dry off. However, as the juice was a red berry blend, the shirt needed to be soaked and washed right away. Mac gave my dad one of his shirts to wear while I dumped my dad's shirt in the washing machine, though it was too loose and hung off my dad's frame.

After the commotion settled, Joshua giggled and giggled, causing the rest of us to join in with laughter.

"Sara, you're always telling me not to spill my milk!" Joshua reminded me, and we all burst into laughter again.

CHAPTER FIFTEEN

Keep on keeping on

BEFORE WE KNEW it, Monday morning was here. The week ahead was fully scheduled, days and evenings alike. Joshua would spend Tuesday, Thursday, and Friday at Marcy's this week while I was teaching. Today, Joshua and I were going to visit a nearby preschool. Mac and I wanted to enrol him in a program that would help him develop his social skills and introduce him to a structured learning environment with children his own age. Classes had already started and most programs were full, thankfully we had found a school a short drive away from our home in a neighbouring community with one space available on Monday and Wednesday afternoons.

Joshua and I arrived at the Creative Kids Preschool twenty minutes before class started. The teacher, Miss Natalie, gave us a tour of the classroom. It was perfect! A large, bright space with a full wall of windows and private entrance to the playground, a comfortable and welcoming environment. Miss Natalie gave me the registration forms to fill out and return to her as soon as possible. I would need to fill out the majority of the paperwork and then obtain signatures needed by the governing department of the Institute of Child Services. Joshua would start class once they approved the program and expenses in approximately two weeks. Though I had originally planned to work with Joshua at home on Monday and Wednesdays, I knew he needed other children in his life besides his daycare friends. Also, as the preschool was only six blocks away from Rockport's most popular park, I planned to take advantage of its running paths until the weather became too frigid.

After supper, Mac and Joshua went outside to do some yard work. They raked up the scattered leaves in the front lawn and tidied up the small perennial garden in the backyard while I busied myself with organizing the next day's events. I picked out my clothes for work and then organized a fall craft for my students to make. I spent some time carefully cutting out large, intricate leaf patterns on red, orange, yellow, and brown paper, which the students would decorate with their names and the added phrase "Be-leaves in God." Finally, I prepped supper for the next night. We had decided to sign Joshua up for indoor soccer, and registration would be taking place at the neighbourhood recreation centre the next day from seven until eight-thirty. Since we usually arrived home around five o'clock on weekdays, supper needed to be somewhat ready so we'd make it in time.

The boys came into the house at seven and we got Joshua ready for bed. We added one more chore routine before turning down the lights; we asked Joshua to pick out his clothes for the next day and place them on the top of the dresser. This would hopefully cut down on the dithering during the morning bustle.

The next day, after a busy school day, I picked Joshua up from Marcy's. A sign on her front door informed parents that her group was at the park down the road at the end of the cul-de-sac. When I arrived at the park, Joshua ran up to me, yelling, "Sara, I missed you!"

Marcy and I often chatted about Joshua's needs and how things were going in general. I'd noticed that his friends would jump into their parents' arms and yell out "Mommy" or "Daddy, I missed you!" when they were picked up. Joshua had begun doing the same thing, which was very sweet, but he looked sad with no one to call "mommy" or "daddy." I decided I would begin to explain the terms "foster mom" and "foster dad" to Joshua soon.

The next day, we received an email from Cassy, and I carefully read the information. She and Rachael would both be attending our next scheduled visit, as they had some items to be reviewed, and some changes to Joshua's family visits to be discussed. I would also be able to pass on the preschool registration to Cassy to submit, for required supervisor signatures.

The day was so busy that Joshua and I made it home from daycare just as Cassy was pulling into the bay, Rachael arriving a minute later. We went inside the house, and I suggested that Joshua, Cassy, and Rachael play air hockey so I could have a minute to change my clothes and put supper in the oven. Joshua and Cassy played an extra hockey game while Rachael and I talked, as I knew Mac would be working late. She told me that Mac and I would need to take a second level care course, as well as a few other training sessions, as required by the Institute of Child Services. I nodded along, but only retained part of the information. Both Mac and I were overloaded with our jobs, parenting Joshua, and keeping up with our own family relationships and matters. The only thing that stuck with me was that we would receive emails sometime soon to sign up for the training sessions and courses.

Joshua and Cassy then joined us at the kitchen table and we talked about Joshua's family visits. They needed to be changed to Tuesdays from four to five o'clock every second week. I felt some rising panic. Neither Mac nor I would be able to take Joshua to these visits, as our work schedules conflicted with this new visit time. However, Cassy stated that she could have a cab hired to take Joshua from Marcy's to the visits. I was hoping Marcy would be okay with this new development. With that, Joshua broke up the quiet conversation.

"Guess what happened?" he blurted.

"What happened?" asked Cassy.

"Sara spilled juice all over her dad at supper and he had to wear one of Mac's shirts! It was too big for him! The juice even got on his socks!"

"Oh my!" Cassy said, raising her eyebrows and laughing.

That night, as I tucked Joshua in, he gazed at my necklace.

"Why do you always wear your cross necklace?" he asked.

"I wear it because it helps me remember that Jesus is always with me when I need him," I said.

"Can I have a cross necklace to wear too?"

"Yes, but you have to take good care of it. Why do you want a cross necklace?" I caressed Joshua's forehead and looked into his eyes.

"I don't want Jesus to forget me, like Nanny and Pops did." Joshua sat up and his upper lip began to quiver.

I remained silent for a few seconds and thought about how to answer his heartfelt words. "Joshua, Nanny and Pops didn't forget you. How about we say a special prayer and ask God for help?"

"Can we ask God right now?"

"Sure, we can ask God every night. God will answer, Joshua, but we need to give him some time to figure it out."

"Okay," he said.

Joshua and I bowed our heads and folded our hands one more time.

"Dear God, we need your help. Joshua is missing Nanny and Pops. What can we do to help Joshua understand that they love him and miss him too? Amen!"

Joshua dropped his head on his pillow and I kissed both of his cheeks. "Goodnight, Joshua."

"Goodnight, Sara."

Joshua watched me as I walked toward the bedroom door. I blew him a kiss and he returned the motion.

CHAPTER SIXTEEN
Deep Discussions

ON SATURDAY, I took Joshua shopping. He had sprouted up like a weed over the summer and needed a full wardrobe. We visited a few children's clothing stores and picked out two sets of pyjamas, socks, and a hoodie with matching sweat pants. It took much longer to find shirts, sweaters, and jeans. Joshua needed to try these items on, and, although he was interested in buying new clothes, he struggled through the process. I guided him gently and complimented him on how handsome he looked after he showed me each item of clothing. One hour later, we both agreed upon three outfits: two pair of jeans and one pair of beige khakis, two long sleeve shirts—one flannel, the other cotton—three t-shirts, and two warm sweaters. Next, we stopped in at the local sporting goods store and purchased two pairs of sneakers for Joshua to wear both indoors at preschool and outdoors.

After a quick stop at home for lunch with Mac, the three of us visited a little shop close to the downtown, which had an assortment of Christian materials, including Bibles, books, and wall decor. We found a children's Bible and a child's cross necklace with the help of the salesperson. I also purchased a story book of "Noah's Ark" with colourful pictures for Joshua.

Back at home, Joshua helped unpack his new clothes and I cut off the price tags. We carefully folded the sweaters, pyjamas, sweat pants, and t-shirts and placed them into the dresser drawers. We hung up the pants, shirts, and hoodie in the closet, and Joshua added his new socks to the sock drawer. Next, we sorted through the clothes that were too small for Joshua.

"Why are we getting rid of these?" Joshua asked.

"We're going to help another little boy who doesn't have nice clothes to wear by giving them away," I said, folding a shirt for the pile.

Joshua looked at me with a puzzled expression. "What other little boy?"

I responded honestly, "I don't know."

Joshua lifted his eyebrows. "Then how do you know a little boy needs my clothes?"

"Well, some mommies and daddies only have enough money to buy food for their kids. They don't have money to buy brand new clothes. There's a very large blue bin near the library where people can drop off the clothes they don't need or wear anymore. Someone picks up the clothes and gives them to other people who need them."

"What's a blue bin?"

"How about we drop the clothes off tomorrow after church, and Mac and I can show you what a blue bin is?"

"Okay." Joshua placed his hands on his hips and shrugged his shoulders.

"Now, how about you pick your favourite items to keep for now?" I suggested.

Joshua picked out a shirt and a pair of pants he couldn't bear to part with. Then Mac and Joshua went downstairs and played with the Lego and Hot Wheels.

That night, we read from Joshua's new Bible. Of course, we started with Genesis 1:1, "In the beginning God created the heavens and the earth." We read until we reached the end of verse 31: "Then God looked over all he had made, and he saw that it was very good! And evening passed and morning came, marking the sixth day." The children's Bible provided a small picture on each page.

"So, God made everything?" Joshua said as we finished reading.

"Yes! Let's read 'Noah's Ark' now. It's one of my favourites!" I replied with delight.

I started reading the storybook quietly, but, when God spoke to Noah, I deepened my voice and spoke with authority. This caught Joshua's attention. He sat up and intensely focused on each picture and part of the story.

"What happened to the people who didn't get on the ark?" Joshua asked as I finished the story.

"They drowned."

"Were they bad people?" Joshua's eyebrows peaked.

"The people that drowned did not obey God; they didn't listen to God." I responded in a matter-of-fact tone.

"Will it ever rain that much here?"

I could see where he was going with this conversation, so I reassured him, "No, God promised that he would never flood the earth again."

Joshua looked a little relieved after hearing this, and he asked me if he could look at the pictures in the book after saying our prayers. I wondered what struck him most about the story.

Sunday morning had us bustling around getting ready for church. Joshua stood in the hallway, watching me curl my hair. I could see his reflection in the large bathroom mirror in front of me. Ever so quietly, I heard him repeating these words: Joshua Jamison, Joshua Jamison, Joshua Jamison. When he stopped, I repeated his full name: Joshua Theodore Sparrow.

"Can I be Joshua Jamison?" he asked.

"No, you're Joshua Theodore Sparrow. You can't be someone else," I said.

"How about Joshua Theodore Sparrow Jamison?" he added.

"No, that won't work either." I didn't say anything more, but realized that Mac and I would need to discuss the concept of foster parents with Joshua very soon. It would be necessary before his next family visit.

After church, we stopped for groceries, and I bought a bag of apples for Joshua to take to his family visit.

"How come you bought more apples? There are so many in the fridge!" Joshua said as we ate lunch.

"I thought it would be nice if you took a bag of apples to your next family visit. Just like when you took the cupcakes for a snack."

"My next family visit?" he asked.

"Yes, you'll go to a visit on Tuesday afternoon. You'll be at Marcy's house so a special driver will pick you up from her house and chauffeur you to the visit."

"What's a chauffeur?" he asked, looking down at the table.

I could tell he was becoming uneasy with the mention of another visit. So, I responded carefully. "A chauffeur is a person who drives you from one place to another. In this case, from Marcy's house to the visit, and then from the visit back to our house. The chauffeur will make sure you're safe in the car. Very important people have chauffeurs."

"I'm important?"

"Yes, you are! Now, eat your pizza."

We began our bedtime routine earlier that night. Mac and I were planning on explaining our role as foster parents to Joshua, but we weren't sure how well he would understand the concept.

Joshua was eager to get ready for bed, as we were going to continue to read from Genesis and re-read "Noah's Ark." He quickly brushed his teeth, put on his new dinosaur pyjamas, and jumped into bed. Joshua snuggled under the warm duvet as we read the story of Adam and Eve. The picture book depicted red fruit that resembled the basic apple, and I could already imagine the questions stirring in Joshua's head. Apples seemed to be the theme of the day!

"Is it bad to eat apples?" Joshua asked after we finished reading the chapter.

"No, the story is just an example of the importance of listening to God, the first time around," I said as I closed the children's Bible.

Joshua sat quiet for a few seconds, then asked one more question. "So, can I still eat apples?"

"Yes."

Next, we read "Noah's Ark." When God spoke to Noah in the story, Joshua asked me to repeat the words over again two times. He was intrigued when I used voice inflections while reading.

After the story, Mac entered the bedroom and sat on the edge of the bed. We explained to Joshua that tonight all three of us would say our prayers together. We bowed our heads and thanked God for his many blessings of family and friends. Then I thanked God for the privilege of being Joshua's foster mom, and for Mac being his foster dad. We ended the prayer with a hearty "Amen." We knew Joshua would ask questions, and we tried to be prepared for his concerns.

"What's a foster mom and foster dad?" Joshua asked.

"A foster mom and dad are parents who look after, love, and provide a safe home for children who need a family. Sometimes for a long time, and sometimes for just a little while." I replied.

Joshua didn't ask anymore questions. We were relieved, but we both knew the subject would come up again.

CHAPTER SEVENTEEN
No Ordinary October

I DROPPED JOSHUA off at Marcy's early Tuesday morning with the big bag of apples for his visit that afternoon. Cassy had sent me an email the day before with the name of the driver who would be picking him up, and given her Marcy's address and contact information. The driver was to provide identification upon pick up. After a quick informational conversation with Marcy about the visit, I gave Joshua a hug and made my way out of the door.

Joshua would be returning home around five-thirty, which gave me a bit of extra time to work in my classroom after school. The beginning of a new month meant new learning themes, and I needed to organize new books, activities, crafts, learning centres, and more. Mac texted me around five o'clock, saying he would be home by five-thirty, so I could work later if I needed and he would look after Joshua. I took advantage of this opportunity and worked until six o'clock.

When I arrived at home, I found Joshua crying in his bedroom.

"What happened?" I asked Mac.

"I'm not quite sure. Joshua came home from his visit upset, but he didn't want to talk about it."

I peeked into Joshua's room. "Are you hungry for supper?" I asked.

He shook his head. "Alright, I'm going to run a bubble bath for you," I said.

I went into the bathroom and began running the water.

"Oh wow, these bubbles are going to overflow. This is the best bubble bath ever!" I said as the tub filled, over-exaggerating the excitement in my voice.

After a moment, Joshua ventured into the bathroom and stood beside me, a half-smile on his face. I helped him into the tub and then plunked myself down on the bathroom floor. Joshua was exhausted and I was concerned that he might fall asleep in the water.

The warmth of the bathroom just about put me to sleep. As Joshua played quietly with the bubbles, I began to ask him about his visit, unsure if he would be able to answer or not.

"Joshua, why were you crying?"

"It was loud at my visit."

"Did you eat an apple at your visit?"

"No." Joshua shook his head and stared down at the bubbles in the water.

"Who was at your visit?"

"Jake, Sean and Anna, and also Miranda, the lady from last time."

"Did they eat apples?"

"Yes, they ate the whole bag full!" Joshua threw his arms up in the air, and water splashed onto the walls surrounding the tub and onto the bathroom floor.

With that we washed Joshua's hair and rinsed off the soap and bubbles. He put on his new flannel soccer pyjamas and combed his hair. He wasn't interested in eating supper, but ate a chocolate pudding for a snack. He went to look at books in his room when he was finished, and, once again, Mac found him asleep with a book on top of his face.

"Did you find out why he was crying? Mac asked me as we got ready for bed that night.

"My best guess is that his visit was confusing. He's spending time with his siblings and biological mother, but he's only seen them a few times over the past few years. They're strangers," I said.

"Yup, that's got to be tough on the little guy. He sure has had a lot of transitions and adjustments in his life over the past while," Mac responded tenderly.

———————

Joshua and I both ended up sleeping longer the next morning, and his mood improved as he played downstairs with the Hot Wheels cars and watched a bit of Treehouse television. I could hear car noises rumbling from his mouth. He must have viewed a commercial advertising Halloween because, the next thing I knew, he came running up the stairs with excitement.

"Sara, Sara, it's almost time to go trick-or-treating!"

Mac and I weren't planning on taking Joshua trick-or-treating, but his next words had me rethinking this decision.

"Nanny and Pops took me. I dressed up like a lion!"

"What would you like to dress up as this year?" I asked.

"A superhero!"

I decided that dressing up as a superhero and knocking on the doors of neighbours for a few pieces of candy and a quick hello would be just fine. "Well, our afternoon is open today, we can go to the department store and see what kind of superhero costumes they have."

"Yay!" he threw up his hands as he cheered.

After lunch, we went shopping for a costume. Joshua admired two costumes in particular: Batman and Spider-man. It was a bit of a toss up, but, after closely inspecting the costumes, he eventually chose Batman because he liked the mask. As soon as we arrived home, Joshua asked me to cut the tags off. He put on the costume and wore it for the remainder of the afternoon.

When Mac arrived home, Joshua bolted to the front entrance and jumped on Mac. "I'm Batman!" he said in a deep voice.

"Hi, Batman! Nice to meet you! Where's Joshua?"

Joshua lifted his mask, "It's me, Joshua, I'm just pretending to be Batman. We went to the big store today and Sara bought a costume for me for Halloween!"

Mac looked at me curiously.

"I'll explain later," I said as I shrugged my shoulders.

"That's a great costume, Joshua!" Mac said, turning back to Joshua. "Batman is a cool superhero; he is a good listener and always does his best!"

"He does?"

"Yes, that's why he's a superhero," Mac said with a nod.

Joshua ran off to play while Mac and I chatted and set the table for supper. I explained Joshua's comment concerning Nanny and Pops taking him trick-or-treating and his lion costume. He had been through more than enough in his short life, and, if trick-or-treating gave him some joy, then so be it. Mac agreed, and we both realized that the Batman costume was likely a bit of an escape from emotional pain for Joshua. Through pretend and play, Joshua could take his mind off his family issues.

Teachers often volunteer for extra-curricular activities, such as coaching sports teams or running student-interest clubs, and I had volunteered to help coach one of the sports teams. We practised during the second half of the lunch hour, which worked well with my schedule and the students. However, games were held after school, and our first game was in two weeks, the same afternoon as Joshua's next family visit. Mac agreed to make sure that he would be home from work to greet Joshua. We circled the date on the calendar so we could properly prepare Joshua for the visit.

The days and following week seem to pass quickly. Once a month, during fall and winter, I volunteered with the sandwich train. A group of us gathered together Friday nights to make sandwiches and coffee and serve them to the inner-city folks. We had a stationary train car equipped with enough seats for twenty, where community members could stop by for food and prayer. For some, this was their only meal for the day, or worse, the entire weekend. Food banks closed over the weekend, and the soup kitchens did the best they could feeding hungry souls.

This weekend was my turn to work with the sandwich train. I left around six-thirty, hoping to be home by midnight. Mac and Joshua made some popcorn and decided to watch *Cars*. I gave Joshua and Mac extended hugs and left for the evening. Joshua was super excited to spend the evening with Mac, eating popcorn, drinking sweet tea with a twirly straw, watching a movie, and getting to stay up late.

Batman woke me up at seven the next morning. There he stood, mask an all, at the side of my bed as I blinked my eyes open. I had gotten home around one o'clock in the morning and fell fast asleep as soon as my head hit the pillow.

I could hear Mac snoring lightly, so I decided to get up and get the day started without disturbing him.

"How was the movie? Were you able to stay awake for all of it?" I asked as Joshua and I sat down to eat breakfast.

"I watched some of it." Joshua ran over to me and gave me a big bear hug. "What are we going to do today?"

"Well, we need to buy you a pair of soccer cleats and shin guards. Your soccer coach sent us an email yesterday, and you'll have your first practice and game combined next Saturday morning at ten. We also need to pick you up a pair of sport shorts."

"But I have shorts!" Joshua's eyebrows tilted as we exchanged comments.

"Do you remember when we dropped off the clothes that didn't fit you anymore into the blue bin?" I rested my elbow on the kitchen table and placed my cheek in my hand.

"Oh yeah. Even my shorts?"

"Yes, even your shorts. They were quite small for you back in the summer, and you've grown taller since then. We'll try to find a basic black pair of shorts. Your coach said that the soccer jerseys are purple and white."

"I love purple!" Joshua responded enthusiastically. "Can I go play with Jasmine today?"

"Yes, when we get home from shopping you can call on her," I said.

"Yay!" he cheered as he ran off to get dressed.

As I stood in the bathroom styling my hair, I felt a presence near me. Sure enough, Joshua had quietly crept down the hallway and was silently watching me. "Sara, what's a real mom?" he asked.

I knelt down so that Joshua and myself were both at eye level. I cupped his face with my hands and waited for a moment before speaking, wondering where this question had come from. "A real mom loves her children unconditionally by telling them very gently what they need to hear, not what they want to hear even when it is difficult or hurts," I began, choosing my words carefully. "A real mom helps her children learn, washes their clothes, tucks them into bed at night, makes their favourite foods to eat, cares for them when they're sick, and misses them when they're not with her. A real mom never gives up on her children when they're going down the wrong path or have been disobedient. A real mom always puts her children before herself and thinks about them often, even when they're all grown up!"

Maybe I went overboard, but I wanted to make sure my answer would work for both me and his biological mom.

"Oh, you're my real mom!" he concluded.

"I guess you could say that, though I'm also your foster mom." I stood up and put my hand on Joshua's shoulder.

"Foster mom? Then who's my real mom?"

I could sense that we were going to go around the mountain a few times with this topic. "Miranda is your tummy mommy; she's your mom too!" I said.

"So, Miranda is my real mom?"

"I am your foster mom, and Miranda is your tummy mommy. You have two real moms. We both love you so much!"

Joshua frowned, and I wasn't sure if he completely understood what I was saying. I wondered if one of the kids at daycare asked him this question and decided to change the topic.

"Guess what? I said.

"What?" Joshua responded with inquisitiveness, tilting his head.

"Your preschool teacher called yesterday and left us a message that you can join class next week! You'll need your very own backpack to take with you to school! We can pick one out today after we purchase your soccer gear."

"Yay! But, Sara, why do I need a backpack?"

"To carry your snack, water bottle, and schoolwork."

"Schoolwork?" Joshua hesitated as he spoke.

"Yes, you'll make beautiful artwork to bring home, and other important work that preschoolers do!"

"Can I get a Batman backpack?"

"Yes, if we can find one."

"Yay!"

I remembered that Joshua wasn't fond of paper and pencil activities, or any work requiring lots of attention. Maybe his own backpack would help give him a boost with confidence or enthusiasm for this new experience.

Joshua and I stopped at a couple of different stores to find his soccer items, but finding a pair of shorts took a bit longer than expected, and we ended up going to a specialized sporting goods store. Next, we went to a big box department store to purchase a backpack. The selection was minimal and picked over. Joshua was disappointed that we couldn't find a Batman backpack. He settled for a *Cars* backpack, as the only other options were plain backpacks of different colours. I thought it was perfect, but Joshua thought it was just okay.

"The characters on the front of the backpack are from the movie you and Mac watched last night!" I said, trying to get him excited.

When we arrived home, Joshua grumpily displayed his soccer gear and backpack for Mac to see.

"Oh cool, a *Cars* backpack! I wish I was going to preschool!" Mac was genuinely excited for Joshua and his upcoming pursuits.

Joshua shrugged his shoulders. His spirits picked up after lunch when Mac and Joshua went outside. He was eager to play with Jasmine, but they only had half an hour before Jasmine had to leave for a diving competition.

Joshua came storming in the front door. Mac soon followed, quite frustrated with Joshua's behaviour and told me that Joshua had a melt down when Jasmine left.

We sent him to his room to sit on the chair beside the desk. He marched his way into the room and let out a forced and bellowing cry. We waited for Joshua to calm down, but he was still worked up fifteen minutes later, so Mac and I entered his bedroom to try and fix the problem.

"I'm going to count to three then you need stop crying and listen with your ears," I said firmly.

I began to count and Joshua slowly stopped crying, though his cheeks were still wet with tears.

"Why are you crying?" I knelt in front of him on the floor.

"I don't know," he sniffed.

"Jasmine went to her diving competition. She played with you until she needed to leave. That was very kind of her," I said with a comforting voice.

"It's not that!" he screwed up his nose.

"Okay then. I need you to sit on the chair for five more minutes and calm down. I'll check on you. If you're ready at that time to come out of your bedroom without screaming, you can help me make jam-jam cookies."

Joshua crossed his arms and averted his gaze. He nodded at me, then Mac and I left him to sit on the chair. When Joshua joined me in the kitchen to bake, we didn't talk about his meltdown and just focused on enjoying our baking. Mac and I understood that the upcoming newness of preschool and soccer, along with added family visits, and daycare, was a heavy load for him.

Joshua and I made a double batch of extra-large cookies. I rolled out the dough and he pressed the star cookie cutter into the dough. After the cookies cooled down, we spread a dollop of jam on the flat side of each and then paired them together. We each ate a cookie for a snack, and then Joshua went downstairs with Mac to build with Lego while I cleaned the kitchen. I purposely set aside a dozen cookies for Joshua's next family visit putting them in a freezer bag and sliding them into the fridge to keep them fresh.,

The remainder of the weekend passed quickly with church, groceries, and Sunday supper. Before we knew it a new week started, launching the three if us into a chain of events that veered into uncharted territory.

On Monday afternoon, I took Joshua to preschool for his class from one to three o'clock. I sent a jam-jam cookie and water bottle with him for snack time, and wrote his name on the inside of his backpack. On our drive over, I played the *Dixie Chicks*, and the two of us sang along to "Taking the Long Way Home," one of Joshua's favourites. By the time we arrived, Joshua was in high spirits and also curious about preschool. His teacher, Miss Natalie, greeted him with a hardy "hello!" and welcomed him to the class. When she introduced Joshua to the other children, they cheered. With all these other kids cheering for him, Joshua smiled at me, and I gave him a big hug.

While Joshua was in class, I went for an hour-and-a-half long walk and run around the city park. Half of the trail paralleled a lake, a simply astounding view! The luscious trees and grass wound up and down grooves on the path. I had forgotten how amazing this space was. The trail was fairly peaceful, with just a few joggers, walkers, and cyclists taking advantage of this sunny and fresh October day. Soon, however, I was on my way back to the preschool to pick up Joshua, waiting with the other parents outside the classroom.

The door opened and, one by one, the children greeted their parents with an excited "Mommy!" or "Daddy!" As he did when I picked him up from daycare, Joshua said my name with affection, but less euphoria.

Once home, Joshua proudly displayed his preschool work: a tree with five branches, three of which had pictures of apples on them that were cut out and pasted. Two of the tree branches were partially coloured brown. A phrase at the bottom of the picture read, "There are five apples on the tree." Joshua's name was printed at the top right hand corner. It was partially completed, but none the less, he was content with his accomplishment. I praised him on his work, and we posted it on the fridge. When Mac arrived home after work, Joshua dragged him over to the fridge to show him his work of the day.

"I like the way you are learning to print your name, very good!" Mac said. Being the husband of a teacher Mac had picked up on how to positively praise young children without being critical. Joshua jumped up and down happily.

Over dinner, Joshua chatted about the kids in his class. He was quite amused that two of the children in the class didn't speak English and that the teacher didn't know what they were saying. The children would point to objects to help the teacher understand or figure out what they were trying to tell her. Then, our conversation changed to Joshua's family visit. We thought we covered everything possible to ensure that he was prepared for it, and he was excited to be taking the jam-jam cookies to share.

I dropped Joshua off at Marcy's with the container of cookies the next morning. The same driver as last time would be picking him up at three-thirty, driving him downtown for his visit, and bringing him back to our house at five-thirty. I would be coaching a soccer game after school, so Mac would be at home to watch Joshua. Everything seemed fine, and I drove to school with confidence. Sort of.

The weather cooperated for our game after school. The two teams warmed up, running drills and taking practice shots on their goalies. Then, a whistle blew, signalling the three-minute warning before the game would begin. The athletes competed, battling up and down the field to score that first point. The teams were evenly matched, and, by half-time, the score was tied two-to-two. At half-time we huddled and talked strategy, then enthusiastically bellowed out our team cheer before re-entering the soccer field. Both teams fiercely competed for the next goal that would break the tie and give advantage to one of the teams.

Ten minutes into the second half of the game, my phone rang. Mac's panicked voice sounded on the other end of the call.

"Hi, Sara, I'm so sorry to interrupt your first soccer game. Joshua just arrived home from his visit, and he's screaming and crying and refusing to get out of the driver's car."

"Oh dear. I'll ask a parent to help the head coach for the rest of the game and I'll be home within fifteen minutes!"

On my drive home, my thoughts scurried back and forth as to what the issue could possibly be. When I pulled up onto the driveway, there was no sign of Mac,

Joshua, or the driver. Mac greeted me as I opened the front door, and I could hear sobs of grief coming from Joshua's room.

"What's up?" I asked with concern.

"As far as I can figure out, Joshua went to some house, and there were people there he did not know. He's upset and keeps telling me he wants to go and live with Miranda."

"Oh dear, I wonder whose house he went to."

"I don't know, but he gave me this crumpled note. It appears to be from Miranda; it's her phone number and a message."

I took the note from Mac and quickly read it over: *Please call me ASAP, Miranda,* with a phone number at the bottom.

It took a couple of hours to calm Joshua down. He refused to eat supper, so I helped him change into his pyjamas and tucked him into bed. I grabbed his children's Bible off the book shelf and looked for a story that would fit our circumstance; we needed a story that included a child and a parent experiencing insurmountable pain and devastation, one that needed Jesus' healing. I flipped to the story of Jarius. His daughter was sick and he heard that Jesus could heal her. However, the girl died before Jesus could reach her. Jarius was very sad, but Jesus told him to have faith and that his daughter would live again. After reading the story, I explained that Jesus could heal Joshua's hurt if we depend on Jesus.

After we prayed for God to heal Joshua's hurt, he gazed at me through his glossy tear- filled eyes and said, "How did Jesus heal the little girl?"

"Jesus spoke words of healing, and the little girl responded to his voice. Jarius, her dad, believed in Jesus."

"I miss Miranda." Joshua sat up. His head drooped down, and large tears rolled down his cheeks.

"I understand. Let's trust Jesus to help." I said. I put my arm around him and held him close.

"How can he help?" Joshua tilted his head toward me, his eyes as big as saucers.

"The Bible says that Jesus is always with us." My eyes met Joshua's, and he gazed at me for a moment.

"But how can Jesus help me?"

"What do you want Jesus to do for you most?" I asked carefully.

"Love me," Joshua responded wearily.

"Jesus loves you, Joshua," I said with certainty.

Joshua lay back down and stared at the ceiling. Then he turned over and hugged his pillow. He didn't ask for a glass of water or anything else that night.

Mac and I sat at the kitchen table that evening, trying to decide what to do about the crumpled note. The only thing we could think of was to ask Cassy if we should call Miranda.

"Do you think we should give Joshua's mom a call?" I asked Mac.

"I don't know," Mac answered, shaking his head. "It would be helpful to have some advice on this one!"

"Yes, I agree!"

It was still and quiet in the house the next morning. I decided to get up and get a few things done before the world and its noise started to sound. I crept by Joshua's room, only to find him awake looking at books on his bed.

"Good morning, you're up very early today. Are you hungry?" I asked, peeking my head through his door.

"Sort of." Joshua shrugged.

"How about I make waffles for you and Mac for breakfast?"

"Yeah!" Joshua cheered.

"Once Mac is awake, I'll call you for breakfast. He's still sleeping because its only six o'clock in the morning, but he'll be up in less than an hour."

I went to the kitchen to complete some paper work for school, pull out something from the freezer for supper, and whip up the waffle batter. Waffles weren't our usual weekday breakfast due to time constraints, but today wasn't a school day for me, so I decided to start the day off with something Joshua really liked.

Mac and Joshua joined me in the kitchen as I had a waffle cooking in the iron.

"Waffles? What's the occasion?" Mac sniffed the air.

"No occasion," I responded, taking the waffle out and adding it to the stack.

After breakfast Joshua returned to his bedroom to get dressed. Mac left for work with an encouraging, "Good Luck!"

At eight o'clock, I called the Institute of Child Services, leaving a long-detailed message regarding Joshua's visit the day before. Next, I got dressed and made my way back to the kitchen to tidy up.

"Joshua, what would you like for snack today at preschool?" I called.

"Bear Paws!" I heard back.

"That sounds yummy!" I said.

Joshua occupied himself all morning with the Lego blocks. While I awaited the return phone call from the Institute of Child Services, I decided to make the most of the morning by writing report card comments for my students, as they were due in a short couple of weeks. Joshua was quietly building structures and creations with the Lego, which was odd for his character. But, after the previous day's events, I decided to chalk it up to internal processing and quiet contemplation.

After a big bowl of chicken noodle soup with soda crackers for lunch, we were on our way to preschool. Instead of my planned run through the park, I went home to call the Institute of Child Services. But, just as I was walking though the door, Mac called me to inform me that he had heard from Cassy, who told him that Joshua's visit had been moved to a different location. The Institute had what they called "family home environments," which were utilized for larger families to provide for more home-like comfort. It seemed that a few more people with whom Joshua wasn't familiar had attended the visit.

I decided to call Cassy to ask a few more questions. After speaking with her, though, I was no further ahead with information, only frustration. She told me that Joshua's visits would now take place in the family house from four to six o'clock. Cassy informed me that these changes were on the agenda for our next home visit with Rachael. She also didn't have an opinion on whether or not Mac and I should call Miranda. I explained the crumpled note once again to her, as Mac did earlier today, but she said the next course of action was up to us.

I thought about her answer for the rest of the afternoon. I decided to ask Joshua a few questions regarding his visit and probe his mind a bit, who knows, maybe he would be able to shed a bit of light on this confusing yet very real dilemma.

When I picked Joshua up from preschool, he was was quiet but happy. Once home, we went downstairs and I pulled out the dollhouse and family figurines, which belonged to our daughters when they were young. As we set the dollhouse up on the carpet, Joshua studied each of the furniture pieces and dolls carefully. I played the mom and dad dolls, and Joshua played the three children and baby figurines. I began to ask a series of questions about his visit.

"Joshua, how did your visit go yesterday?" I asked.

"Good," he responded using the boy figurine.

"Who was at your visit?" I placed the mother doll face to face with the boy figurine Joshua was holding.

"Miranda, my brothers and sisters, and uncle Mason, and auntie Georgina, and I think that's all."

"Oh wow, that's a lot of people!"

"Everybody was talking!"

"Why were you crying when you came home?" I sat the doll on the mini couch and looked at Joshua.

"I was sad because I wanted to stay with my mom. She said I'm her baby and that she wanted her kids to come and live with her." Joshua picked up the baby doll and placed it into the arms of the mother doll.

"I see. Well, Mac and I are going to phone Miranda and try to figure out how to make your visits happy," I said.

Joshua continued to play with the dollhouse set, and I went upstairs to make supper; he didn't look up when I left the room. When Mac arrived home from work, we discussed the possibility of a phone call to Miranda. We decided to place a call to Miranda on Sunday afternoon.

At our visit with Rachael, Mac and I brought up our concerns over the lack of communication about changes to Joshua's visits. Rachael told us that sometimes the changes were made to accommodate the foster child's biological family and that the foster family is not necessarily privy to this information. Mac and I thought this odd, especially since Joshua and his siblings were considered permanent wards of the Institute.

On Saturday, we had Joshua's first soccer practice and game in the morning. We walked into the gymnasium filled with children, parents, and grandparents. After helping Joshua put on his shin pads and cleats, Mac and I climbed the stairs to the bleachers to watch the game. The coach was the mom of a little girl on our team, and Joshua took a liking to her immediately. After a thirty-minute practice, the teams engaged in an entertaining game. The little players needed to learn the skill of running in the right direction and often bunched up in a herd after the soccer ball, accidentally kicking each other instead of the ball. The goal tenders became distracted and occasionally wandered away from their net to talk with other players sitting on the bench, waiting their turn to play.

Joshua was excited after the game to go shopping for a brand-new Hot Wheels car as a reward for doing his best, and we congratulated him on a good game.

"Did we win?" he asked.

"Yes!" we said, even though nobody kept score.

On Sunday afternoon, I called Miranda, Mac and Joshua sitting at the kitchen table with me.

"Hello," she answered on the second ring.

"Hi, is this Miranda?" I said. Joshua and Mac sat very patiently, looking at me.

"Yes, who is this?"

"This is Sara, Joshua's foster mom." Joshua moved closer to me and leaned in to my side, resting his head on my shoulder.

"Oh! I'm so happy you called me!" Miranda said, her voice softening.

"My husband Mac and I thought we should talk to you about how to make things easier on Joshua."

"I appreciate it so much; I miss him dearly, and I don't know anything about where my children are living."

"Joshua has a good home with us. We love him just as if he was one of our own children. But he seems to be getting upset after his family visits. We're hoping weekly group conversations with Mac, Joshua, you, and me will help him through his hurt feelings."

"That sounds like a great idea. It's so hard on all of us to visit for such a short period of time. Before we know it, it's time to go and we hug and cry together."

"I understand," I said. "I think if you have the opportunity to talk with him weekly, you could both share more about what's going on with every day life and build a relationship. Perhaps then the visits will be happier."

"Yes, I completely agree," Miranda said.

"Do Sunday afternoons work for you?" I asked.

"Yes, that's perfect!"

"Would you like to speak with Joshua?" I said. "I can put him on speaker phone."

"I would love that."

I passed the phone to Mac, and he pressed the speaker button on the phone. We helped guide Joshua through his conversation with his mom. He was timid, but answered Miranda's questions with our assistance. He told her about his soccer game the day before, Sunday school, and that he was going to be Batman for Halloween next week. Miranda was encouraging and supportive. After one hour of phone conversation, we all said our goodbyes. This was the beginning of our weekly chats. First, Joshua would chat with his mom for a while, then Miranda and I would talk. This was also the start of a unique friendship between myself and Miranda, one that I never could have imagined.

That evening, Joshua and I completed his bedtime routine with a sense of content. We read a chapter from, his Bible, re-read "Noah's Ark," and prayed with one addition to Joshua's prayer request. We prayed that Joshua would one day be able to live with his mom.

———————

Our final activity of the month was Halloween. Our plan was to have Mac hand out candy at our house while I walked Joshua around the bay and over to a couple of friend's houses a few blocks away. But, on the day of, we were all extremely tired. It was a school day for me and a childcare day for Joshua. By the time we got home, ate supper, and put Joshua's Batman costume on, it was already after six-thirty in the evening. I could tell Joshua was tired by the way he leaned on his elbow while trying to eat supper.

Off Joshua and I went to collect a few treats and say hello to the neighbours. Joshua tripped on his way down our front steps. I wasn't sure if it was because he couldn't see clearly out of his mask or if his tiredness was gaining momentum. We walked slowly around the bay and up to each door. Joshua's voice was barely able to call out "Trick or treat!" so he ended up knocking on doors instead. I stood on the sidewalk, waving to our friends and neighbours who opened the door.

We finished the last home on our bay, and Joshua decided he wanted to continue for a bit longer. We trudged over to Laura and Blake's house a few blocks away. But, before long, Joshua stumbled and blew a shoe, scattering his pumpkin and its contents. He sat on the sidewalk, put his shoe on, and picked up his candy, and we carried on in silence. Laura didn't recognize Joshua in his Batman costume, and he didn't tell Laura who he was, perhaps because he was exhausted. I texted her on our walk back home, and she was surprised she hadn't recognize him at all.

Finally, we arrived back at our bay, and Joshua stumbled one more time, dumping his candy all over our neighbour's grass. We picked up as much as we could find, but I was certain the neighbour would find a few treats strewn about his lawn in the morning.

CHAPTER EIGHTEEN
such is Life

NOVEMBER WAS ALWAYS a busy month for me at school. Report cards, parent teacher conferences, and Christmas concert practices all needed extra time and attention.

We continued our scheduled visits with Cassy and Rachael. Joshua looked forward to preschool afternoons, and we found that his social skills were improving. We enjoyed our routine of daycare, Saturday soccer, church and Sunday school, weekly phone calls to Miranda, and family visits.

We created a special photo album with photos of Joshua's life and chose four pictures for Joshua to give to his mom during his next visit: a picture of himself fishing off of our dock at the cottage, one of him sitting on his bike on the bay, an action shot of him kicking the soccer ball, and a photo of him wearing his Batman costume.

Joshua and I baked chocolate chip cookies the day before his next visit and filled a large plastic Tupperware container with two dozen cookies. I was certain that the cookies would be devoured. Mac and I prepared Joshua for the visit, covering where it would take place and who might be there. We discussed behaviour and appropriate manners, as well as reassured him that we all loved him and that this would not be his last visit with his mom.

Joshua was to be picked up as usual at Marcy's by three-thirty. At four, I received a call at school from Marcy, who told me that Joshua's driver didn't show up. I quickly called Cassy to let her know and find out what happened. Apparently, Joshua's driver was ill, but no one had informed us or Joshua's biological family. Therefore, Marcy was left hanging, waiting by her front door with Joshua and the other daycare children who would always see Joshua off and then return to their planned activity. Cassy immediately organized a taxi to pick Joshua up and extended his visit by an hour so he could visit with his family. When I called Miranda to let her know the situation, she was very upset. By the time Joshua arrived, he only had one hour to visit with his siblings as they were being picked up to go back to their foster homes as scheduled, but he was still able to visit with his mom.

However, when he returned home at seven, Joshua said, "My dad was at the visit."

"What?" Both Mac and I responded in unison.

"I saw my dad."

Mac and I looked at each other, not knowing how to respond. We were thankful that Joshua wasn't crying, but his mood was a bit unsettled. He hadn't seen his biological father for at least a couple of years.

"Are you hungry?" I asked. We'd already eaten supper.

"A little bit," Joshua replied.

"Alright, go and wash up and I'll heat up some lasagne for you."

Joshua was very hungry; he ate quickly and guzzled a big glass of milk.

"My dad says that we're his people," Joshua said after as he ate a chocolate chip cookie for dessert.

"Do you mean family?" I asked

"He said me and my brothers and sisters, and my mom and him, are my people." Joshua crossed his arms and stood straight.

"Oh, I see," I said, facing Joshua and feeling my body tense up. I stood frozen, overwhelmed and unsure of what else to say.

We completed our bedtime routine quietly and included Joshua's dad, Theodore Sparrow, in our prayers. Joshua didn't show a great deal of emotion for him, and didn't mention him again for the next two weeks.

Our weekly Sunday afternoon conversation with Miranda cleared up a few uncertainties. Theodore was back in her life. They each had their own separate living arrangements for now, but they were looking for a bigger place to move in together with Miranda's older children, who would be released into her care within the next three to six months if she completed parenting courses and passed the Institute's regulations. It would not be an easy journey, however, Miranda struck us as the type of person who would do what she had to do to get her family back, so as to speak. Miranda was bold, opinionated, and determined. She was also passionate about her children, and her love for all of them was obvious.

Over the next two weeks, we dealt with unusual and odd behaviours from Joshua. Marcy also experienced strange outbursts from Joshua at daycare; he became obstinate and at times had tantrums. The only change in his life was the appearance of his biological father. We decided to bring this up at our next meeting with Rachael.

"Sometimes children act out or have a hard time dealing with their emotions when a family member—in this case being Joshua's biological father—is reintroduced into their life," she said.

"Who made the arrangements for this involvement and why weren't we informed that Joshua's father would be attending the visit?" I asked, accentuating my words and frowning.

"We aren't required to inform foster families of these changes, and, in this case, it was out of our control. A court order permitted Joshua's father to attend the visit."

"Well, it's difficult to prepare Joshua for his visits when we don't know who'll be attending them," Mac said.

"I understand," Rachael said. "It's probably safe to say that Joshua's father will be in attendance at family visits from here on out."

December arrived and, with it, the holiday season. With Joshua's family visits and meetings with the Institute of Child Services, as well as the travel documentation required for out of county travel with foster children, we decided to lie low and celebrate the holiday quietly.

Joshua and I were busy baking on the weekends and wrapping Christmas gifts for our loved ones. We had gone shopping and picked out gifts for his family members: a housecoat and bath products for Joshua's mom; chocolates and socks for his dad; earrings and manicure sets for his sisters; and winter gloves and chocolates for his brothers.

The Institute planned a special Christmas visit on the Saturday before Christmas for Joshua and his family to spend the afternoon together. We decided to bake and decorate a gingerbread house for Joshua to share with his family.

We also decorated our home with a Christmas tree, white lights, and colourful decorations. I hung a wreath on the front door and set a Christmas tablecloth and centrepiece on the kitchen table. I poured a special fragrance of patchouli and myrrh oil into a specially-made brass holder and set it on the coffee table in the living room. Lastly, we put a nativity scene on the hearth of the fireplace, along with beaded garland that stretched from end to end of the mantel. Joshua wanted a decoration for his bedroom, so I retrieved a gift given to me by one of my students years ago: a stuffed reindeer with light-up antlers and a button that played "Rudolph the Red-Nosed Reindeer." He kept it on top of the dresser across from his bed.

One early December morning, while I was styling my hair for work, Joshua appeared in the bathroom door and asked, "Are you going to wear perfume today?"

"No, I only wear perfume when Mac and I go out somewhere special. We're not allowed to wear perfume at school."

"Why?"

"It bothers some people," I answered as best I could without a long explanation of school regulations and rules. Then I got a whiff of patchouli. I couldn't figure out why it was so strong in the hallway. As Joshua came closer to give me a hug, the scent became stronger! I looked down to see his hair was shiny with oil.

"Did you rub patchouli oil in your hair?" I asked.

"How can you tell?" he said, looking up at me.

"I can smell it!"

"I wanted to smell good," he replied.

I sighed and shrugged my shoulders. There was nothing I could do about the oil soaking into Joshua's head at the moment. We would need to wash it out tonight when I came home from work. Oil wasn't easy to wash out, and I knew Joshua would probably smell like a Christmas candle for a week.

Marcy planned a festive Christmas party for her daycare children. The children drew names from a red Christmas stocking and exchanged gifts. Marcy also purchased a gift for each child, and Joshua was ecstatic to receive a remote-controlled monster truck. He, in turn, gave Marcy a gift card to one of her favourite stores and a scented hand soap.

Joshua's preschool was winding down for the two-week Christmas holiday break. Each afternoon he attended preschool, the class made a special craft. Joshua brought home his crafts, and we displayed them on the side of the fridge with magnets.

Joshua's family Christmas visit arrived, and he was excited to give each family member their special gift. Cassy picked him up with the promise to return him by six o'clock. Mac and I gave him a big hug and reassured him that he would have a wonderful time with his family. We kept our additional feelings to ourselves, not quite certain of the frame of mind Joshua would be in when he returned to our home.

Mac and I enjoyed our quiet afternoon together, running a few errands, wrapping our Christmas gifts for Joshua, and taking a late-afternoon nap. We ordered pizza for supper from our favourite restaurant, along with an individual cheese pizza for Joshua in case he was hungry when he got home.

Cassy and Joshua arrived right on time at six o'clock. Joshua rang the door bell, which was odd as he usually walked right in. We greeted him with smiles and hugs, but he backed off a little bit. Cassy said that he had a nice time at his visit and that he fell asleep in her car on the way home. He held a gift bag in his hand, containing one of his favourite stuffed animals from when he was a baby, which he immediately set on his bed.

"We ordered pizza for supper, are you hungry?" I asked as Joshua joined us in the kitchen.

"A little bit," Joshua muttered.

"Go wash up and I will warm it up for you," I said, taking the pizza out of the fridge.

Joshua ate one piece of cheese pizza and then declared that he was full. "When do I get to go back to Nanny and Pops' house? I miss them," he said as he finished supper.

I exchanged a surprised glance with Mac. Joshua hadn't mentioned Steve and Jan for quite a while now, and we were expecting him to bring up his mom again. After Joshua fell asleep, I called Jan. We discussed a possible visit with her and Steve in the near future. Jan was happy to hear that Joshua thought of them and she expressed how much they missed Joshua. Being the Christmas season, Jan and Steve thought it would be nice to have a holiday visit with Joshua. That being agreed upon, we planned the visit for the next Monday afternoon from one to five o'clock.

On Sunday night, as Joshua got ready for bedtime, I asked him to pick out a nice outfit for the next day and hang it on the closet door.

"Are we going somewhere special?" he asked, raising his eyebrows.

"Mac and I aren't, but you are," I said with a smile.

"Where am I going?"

"Nanny and Pops are coming to pick you up to have a visit with them!"

Joshua gasped and cheered. He picked out a pair of khaki pants, t-shirt and sweater to wear for the next day, and I pulled out his matching lower cut dress boots.

When the doorbell rang the next day, Joshua swung open the door to find Nanny and Pops on the front stoop. He jumped into their arms for big hugs and then put on his winter gear. He grabbed both of their hands and happily walked out of the front door.

At five o'clock Joshua walked back in the front door with a giant grin on his face. We exchanged gifts of chocolates with Steve and Jan, and Joshua showed us his new pair of sunglasses, Lego, Hot Wheels car, and yo-yo. Joshua gave Nanny and Pops hugs and kisses, and then they left. This was the last time he would ever see them again. As time went on, Joshua did not mention their names again. In his heart and mind, he seemed to have closure of a life once lived and loved.

———————

The day before Christmas Eve, Mac planned to slip out to the hardware store to pick up a few items he needed for a wood working project.

Joshua asked if he could tag along. "Can I go with you?" Mac was standing in the front porch, already dressed in his winter gear and getting ready to leave. "Please, please!" Joshua said.

I heard Joshua's request from the kitchen and joined them at the entrance. "Would it be okay if we both join you?" I asked. "We are getting a little stir crazy inside the house, and an outing would break the day up."

Mac was not overly excited about the idea. "I was just going to go in and out of the store quickly."

"We won't bother you, we can look around while you gather your items," I remarked. Joshua reached for Mac's hand and jumped up and down.

Mac sighed and gave in, "Hurry up, and put your coats on, I'll warm up the car."

At the store, Joshua and I wandered, gazing at the Christmas displays. We came upon a remote control Christmas train and track. Joshua used the hand control system to move the train forward and backward on the track. He pressed every button, initiating train sounds and popular Christmas tunes! We stood there playing with it for quite some time.

Mac's voice piped up from behind us. "There you are; I've been looking for you both. I have my supplies, let's go home."

I smiled at Mac and pointed at the track, indicating that I wanted to buy it.

He held up his hands in surrender and said, "I'm only agreeing because I want to get home."

Mac and I lifted the large and heavy box onto the bottom tray of the shopping cart. Joshua cheered loudly, "Yay!"

At home, we set up the track in the living room, and Joshua played with it for hours!

––––––––––––

Christmas day arrived. I was up early, preparing a feast for our small and intimate Christmas celebration with my dad, Tess, Mac, Joshua, and me.

Joshua must have heard me in the kitchen, the clanging of pots and pans and Christmas music. Or, maybe he awoke excited to find Santa's presents under the tree.

"There are more presents under the tree! And the cookies and milk are gone!" he shouted as he ran into the kitchen.

"Wow! That's awesome!" I turned around and hugged Joshua tightly.

I knew he wouldn't be able to sit through breakfast knowing that Santa had made a stop at our house to deliver presents to him. So, Tess and I made ourselves coffees while Mac made some hot cocoa, and then Joshua led the way to the living room. Joshua opened his gifts, squealing with jubilation with every gift he unwrapped, excited to find that Santa had delivered every item on his list. We were all blessed.

CHAPTER NINETEEN
The Heart of Winter

IN JANUARY, TESS signed up to play recreational hockey, which nudged me into purchasing a pair of skates and a helmet for Joshua. Our entire family enjoyed playing hockey in winter, and our community hockey rink offered one free night of skating per week. This was the perfect opportunity to introduce Joshua to skating.

The weekend before I had to go back to school, Tess had her first hockey game, and my dad, Mac, Joshua, Tydon, and I went along as fans in the stands. We found seats on the inside, right in front of the glass window. Our stools were quite tall, but we sat ourselves down and waited for the puck to drop. Joshua was quite distracted by everything around us. He continuously climbed off an on his stool. As he tried to climb on his stool, it tipped towards the glass and he flew forwards. He raised his arms and dropped to the floor. Tydon reached him just in time to help him up, and we all stared at Joshua, astonished and thankful that he wasn't hurt.

"I'm okay!" Joshua said.

We burst into laughter, more out of relief than humour. In any case the hockey game was exciting and we all had a wonderful family night out.

Tydon left after lunch the next day, and we sat down with Tess. We put a movie on for Joshua in the basement and the three of us gathered at the kitchen table, sipping peach tea. Tess told us that she had decided to finish her nursing degree. The look on her face gave way to something that perhaps could be expected, but not quite prepared for.

"That's a smart decision. Which campus are you thinking about enrolling in?" I asked.

Tess hesitated for a moment, but then smiled. With excitement in her voice, she replied, "Douglas College in Foxpine!"

"That's great news that you have been accepted into Douglas! Your mom and I are so proud of you! You're a young adult with a life of your own. We will support your educational decision with anything you need." Mac gave Tess a long hug.

"I'm already missing you and you're standing right in front of me!" I smiled and cried at the same time. "Your dad and I have noticed that you and Tydon have a close relationship. He's a wonderful young man!"

Tess shared with us that she and Tydon had talked about marriage and their future together. It made sense for her to continue and finish nursing school in the county where she planned to live in the future.

Mac and I were happy for her, but Tess being our last child to leave home would also be difficult for us. We were thankful for the days we had with our children and the memories captured by our family photos on the walls.

It was at our next in-home visit with both Cassy and Rachael, almost two weeks into the month of January, that they told us permanent placement procedures were moving forward for Joshua and some of his siblings. We were surprised because family visits had continued, and we weren't sure whether or not Miranda and Theodore knew about this decision. None of our conversations with Miranda indicated she or Theodore were aware of this development.

Cassy and Rachael told us that we would need to complete a number of tasks for Joshua's permanent placement by the second week of February. First, Joshua was to have a complete physical check-up. Next, we would have to get his bloodwork done. And, finally, we were to select a nice photo of Joshua for his placement profile dossier. We added this to our list to do and carried on with life's more pleasant events.

Our first skate with Joshua was challenging to say the least. Mac and I took turns supporting him from behind. He often flopped down or lost balance quickly when we encouraged him to shuffle skate on his own. We knew this activity would provide some frustration for Joshua, and he soon learned that there would be no option to quit or give up. We rewarded him with a cup of hot cocoa with mini-marshmallows once we arrived home.

Saturday soccer rewarded Joshua with a nice surprise. He received the player of the game award, which included a gift card for a pita sandwich and a beverage, as well as a certificate. We used the gift card immediately after the game, as we weren't sure how much more time Joshua would be with us and we didn't want to forget about it once the hectic work week started again. We set his certificate in a frame and hung it on the bedroom wall. Joshua's smile stretched from ear to ear. He asked if he could go next door and invite Jasmine over to see it. We agreed, and soon the two kids were having fun playing a game of air hockey in the basement.

After church on Sunday, we shopped for groceries and picked out two cakes for Joshua's upcoming birthday. Joshua would be taking one of the cakes to his family visit and the other one was for his birthday party the next Saturday afternoon. After putting all of the groceries away, we had lunch and called Miranda. Joshua was eager to tell her all about his soccer award and the birthday cake he was bringing to the family visit.

"I played soccer and we won! I got a special prize too!"

"That's good to hear. I love you so much!" Miranda responded.

Joshua grinned ear to ear.

Miranda and Joshua enjoyed their conversation together, and then Mac and I spoke with Miranda. We were surprised to find out that Theodore was now living with Miranda again. They had found a small house close to the downtown. Miranda's oldest child was also living with them. Theodore asked to speak with his son.

"Joshua, my son, I'm so proud of you learning to skate. Maybe you will be a great hockey player one day."

Joshua nodded with his head. I whispered to Joshua to answer with, "Yes I am," but all that came out of his mouth was a very soft "uh-huh."

"I'll see you soon, my boy!"

Joshua looked at Mac and me, expressionless. Mac looked at Joshua and silently mouthed "Say 'goodbye,'" which Joshua mumbled back to his dad.

Miranda and I finished the phone conversation. I confirmed that Joshua was bringing birthday cake to their family visit this week, as well as party favours, paper plates and plastic forks. Miranda was appreciative, her voice however seemed quivery and had a sad tone to it. Miranda explained that she and Theodore were trying to do everything possible to gain back custody of their children. I responded with encouragement, knowing that plans were being made for permanency by the institute. I suggested that perhaps she and Theodore could set up a meeting with the Institute of Child Services to understand the situation more completely.

January seemed to roll along. Living with uncertainty became routine for us. Joshua was happy to share birthday cake with his family. He mentioned that his dad and two of his sisters were absent, but he didn't seem to be to concerned, he was mostly happy just to visit with his mom.

Marcy celebrated Joshua's birthday at daycare by serving his favourite meal for lunch and cupcakes for snack. The small group of children sang "Happy Birthday" and cheered for him.

On Saturday after soccer, Mac, my dad, Tess, Jasmine, and I went to McDonald's for lunch at Joshua's request. After munching down the burgers, Joshua and Jasmine played on the structure at the play area. We enjoyed birthday cake back at our house, and Joshua opened his gifts from us: a large firetruck, a box of Lego, and a package of twenty Hot Wheels cars that came with a track.

CHAPTER TWENTY
Happy Hearts, Hurting Hearts

FEBRUARY WAS THE month I liked to celebrate friendship in my classroom. With St. Valentine's Day on the calendar, my students and I exchanged cards and had a Valentine's party.

Joshua would also be having a party at his preschool, so the two of us visited the dollar store and picked out Valentine's cards to exchange with his classmates. I picked out puppy and kitty cards for my students, and Joshua picked out superhero cards for his friends. We spread out our cards on the kitchen table and addressed them to each individual, signing our names at the bottom. I helped Joshua with each of his classmates' names, and he printed his own name independently. This was an enormous task for Joshua, and I rewarded him with mini marshmallows after each card he completed.

Later in the week, Joshua had appointments at the doctor and the medical lab. The doctor listened to Joshua's heart and looked in his ears. I felt a little angry when the doctor asked me right in front of Joshua the reason for the check-up and the bloodwork, and I hoped Joshua wouldn't catch my answer. I answered the doctor with two words, "permanent placement." The doctor acknowledged my response with a quick nod of his head.

On our drive home, Joshua asked me why I took him to the doctor.

"Just to make sure you're healthy!" I said.

"Am I?" he asked with a smile.

"Yes, you're super healthy!" I smiled back.

Mac accompanied us to the lab appointment later. I didn't want to take Joshua by myself, just in case things didn't go smoothly. I hadn't said anything to Joshua about this appointment because I didn't want him to be afraid. Joshua happily plunked himself down into the chair when the lab technician asked him to.

"Can you roll up your sleeve for me?" the technician asked.

"Why?" asked Joshua.

"I need to see your arm."

"Okay," Joshua said. He bunched up his sleeve at his shoulder.

"Now, this might pinch a bit," the technician said as he held up the fine needle to Joshua's arm.

Joshua stiffened in his chair and looked at me with a panicked expression. I quickly told the lab technician that I hadn't told Joshua what was going to happen at this visit.

The lab technician glanced at me quickly, then back at Joshua. "I see. Well, I wonder what colour your blood is. Blue, maybe green?" he said.

Joshua shrugged his shoulders.

"Do you want to find out?" the technician said, raising his eyebrows and smiling.

Once again, Joshua shrugged his shoulders, but gave a curious nod and watched as the technician stuck the needle into his arm. He didn't budge or say a word.

"Wow, it's red blood!" the technician said.

Joshua smiled and he picked out a superhero band-aide.

"That hurt!" Joshua said, once we were on our way home.

"Really? You were so brave!" I said.

"I'm going to go and get David and we are going to fly away in a hot air balloon!"

Mac and I looked at each other puzzled. But, after thinking about it for a moment, I wondered if Joshua was making it clear that he wasn't going to let this type of painful activity happen to my dad. Joshua was very fond of my dad, and it was nice to know he didn't want him to be the victim of any unforeseen needles in the future.

———————

One Saturday after soccer, Mac and Joshua decided to build a snow fort on the island in the middle of our bay with Jasmine. I peeked out of the front door and saw they had built quite the structure! The snow fort looked like a medieval castle. Jasmine's dad had given them a board for the entrance and they placed lawn chairs on the top level of the fort. Jasmine had retrieved a flag from her basement storage room and they stuck it at the very top of the fort. A few minutes later, Joshua burst through the front door, crying, the right side of his face scratched and bleeding.

"What happened?" I asked.

"Glen was pulling the kids in a saucer sled behind his quad," Mac said, showing up behind Joshua. "They weren't going very fast, so Jasmine and Joshua called out for Glen to go faster. When he did, Joshua let go of the saucer handles, fell out, and rolled out onto the road."

"Why did you let Joshua ride in the saucer?" I said, my voice raising. "You know he's clumsy with new activities. He should have had a helmet on!"

"He's okay. They weren't going that fast," Mac said, frowning at me. "It's just a scratch. He's more shaken up about tumbling out."

"I sure hope it heals before his next visit!" I bent down to examine the scratch on Joshua's cheek.

"It will, it's just a small scratch," Mac said. He took a tissue out of his coat pocket and wiped Joshua's nose.

We were glaring at each other when we noticed that Joshua had stopped crying and was staring at us. He had never seen us upset with each other or raise our voices. I quickly apologized for raising my voice and making a big issue out of nothing. I wondered if Joshua had memories of his biological parents in heated discussions or other.

"Can I go back outside and play?" Joshua asked.

"You can once you wash your face," Mac said.

Ten minutes later, Mac and Joshua were back outside. Jasmine and Joshua went back to playing in their fort, and I brought them two Styrofoam cups of hot chocolate and cookies for a snack. The incident was forgotten.

On Sunday afternoon, Joshua and I baked heart cookies to bring to his next family visit, and we called Miranda to tell her all about it. Joshua told her all about the activities and excitement in his life over the past couple of weeks.

Then, Miranda told me about the educational courses she was taking in order to get her high school diploma. She was meeting with family support workers and other professionals who had expertise with regaining custody of children in the system. She was also mentoring another young mom who had lost her children due to drug and alcohol addictions. I thought this was amazing. Miranda was working very hard at putting all the pieces of her life back together so she could put her family back together.

At our next meeting with Cassy, she told us that Joshua's results from his health check were in and all was good. She needed a picture for his personal portfolio, so we went through the photo album we were creating for Joshua to keep. Joshua and Cassy perused over every picture. Cassy asked Joshua if she could keep one of the pictures. He was delighted, and they selected a picture of him holding the firetruck he received for his birthday.

Joshua was more quiet than usual when he returned home from his next family visit. I asked if they enjoyed the heart shaped cookies and Joshua nodded.

"I want to live with my mom!" he blurted out, his eyes filling with tears.

"I see. How about we pray about it and ask God for help?" I said, folding my hands together.

Through streaming tears and a muffled "okay," Joshua got ready for bed. Once tucked into bed, we read "Noah's Ark," which Joshua was now able to recite from memory. Then we prayed for Joshua and his family to be together again, to be a family once more.

Sunday's weekly afternoon phone call to Miranda caught me off guard. Usually, Miranda was very eager to talk with Joshua for a while, but she began this conversation by talking to me.

"I want to ask you a question," she said.

"What's on your mind?"

"Are you planning on adopting Joshua?"

My jaw dropped. "No, we're in no position to adopt Joshua," I said. "But, permanent placement plans have gone ahead for your younger children. I wasn't sure if you and Theodore knew about this."

Miranda sighed. "Our support worker just told us. She said plans were being made to place all of the children in permanent custody."

"Miranda, that doesn't mean you stop fighting for your children," I said, my voice soft and comforting. "Keep communicating with the Institute. Your children will see your relentless determination and love for them, even in the midst of their custody and placement procedures. Continue making your own life one of examples to others. I can pray with you too, if you would like."

"Thank you, I need the encouragement. I'm trying so hard to get my life together and provide a home for my kids."

"I know, Joshua always asks to come and live with you," I said. "He loves you very much."

We ended our conversation in prayer.

CHAPTER TWENTY-ONE
April Showers, May Flowers, and Mud

WINTER TURNED TO spring. Birds tweeted their sweet songs early in the morning. The longer days gave us more daylight time to accomplish outdoor jobs. It also meant that Joshua's bedtime was a little later. We were all spending a lot more time outside, enjoying the warmth of spring. Soccer ended, as well as skating sessions, but Joshua was happy just to have free time to play outside.

Joshua's visits continued with his family. Miranda and I spent time talking on the phone every Sunday. She had recruited a family lawyer through the government. who would represent her case with no fee requirement. She and Theodore both had to complete a variety of family courses and several volunteer-work projects in their community, and so, they were painting the neighbourhood family centre downtown. Miranda was also applying for work and had three upcoming interviews. They were certainly making positive changes in their lifestyle.

By the beginning of April, the snow was gone and the roads were dry, except for across the bay where the road had a dip in front of the sidewalk and water collected to form a rather large puddle. One day, as Joshua went outside to ride his bike, I noticed the giant puddle across the street.

"Joshua, don't ride your bike through puddles, especially the one across the street. It's very deep, and you'll get wet, and then you'll have to come back inside the house," I said.

Joshua looked at me, but didn't respond as he ran out the door. Joshua was wearing waterproof splash pants and a windbreaker, but his socks and runners would get wet if he rode his bike through the puddle. Fifteen minutes later, Joshua was crying at the front door. He was soaked from head to toe, hair and all.

"What happened?" I asked, raising my voice and crossing my arms.

"I fell off my bike." Joshua looked down at his feet.

"How did you get all wet?" I responded.

"I was riding through the puddle," he mumbled.

"I see. Well, I need you to come inside now," I said.

Joshua sniffed as tears leaked from his eyes.

"First, you didn't listen when I asked you to stay out of the puddles," I said. "Second, you're soaking wet and need to change into dry clothes. I can put your splash pants and jacket in the dryer, but your runners will need to dry on their own."

Joshua dragged his feet as he came inside, but he knew that, because he rode through the deep puddle of water, he would have to spend the rest of the day inside the house.

One night after supper, Mac and Joshua headed outside to work in the garage. Mac found our children's go-kart in the attic and taught Joshua how to ride it. It didn't take much to learn how to steer and stop the go-kart. Joshua soon learned how to slam on the breaks and hurdle the go-kart into a sideways stop, or leave a long skid mark on the sidewalk or road. Joshua enjoyed this new outdoor activity and spent hours ripping around the bay.

April showers continued on and off, making it challenging for Joshua to escape outside, though not for lack of trying. As usual, Mac would work on a project after supper and Joshua would attempt to go for a spin on his bike or the go-kart, only to encounter sprinkles of rain or an out-right down pour. In late April, the rain seemed to last forever. Though the grass and trees were benefiting greatly, and the flowers were blooming, it also brought endless loads of wet laundry. Joshua found the many puddles tempting, and he couldn't find the will power to avoid them. I often found him crying at the front door, soaked from head to toe. He knew the drill: change into dry clothes and wait for the foot wear to dry, then repeat the process. I never asked him what happened, but he would recount every time he rolled through the puddle across the street in detail. Though I had purchased Joshua a pair of rubber boots, he always managed to tumble into the puddles in such a way that the water filled the insides. Nothing could keep him from riding through the puddles. We would just have to be patient and wait out the rainy weather.

CHAPTER TWENTY-TWO
Triumphs and Tribulations

IN MAY, JOSHUA was invited to his first birthday party for a little girl from daycare. The party was to be held at a hotel pool with a water slide. Joshua was excited, but hesitant, as he remembered the ride down the water slide at the hotel in Barrington from our family trip the summer before. Mac and I were hoping that he would overcome this fear, but he seemed to hang onto it, so, Mac and I decided to enrol Joshua in swimming lessons. We wanted him to feel comfortable and practice safety in the water, whether he was water-sliding or participating in water activities at the lake.

One morning, as I was getting ready for the day, I noticed that Mac's and my toothbrushes had dried gobs of toothpaste on them. Joshua's toothbrush always had toothpaste remnants stuck on the brush. He was always in too much of a hurry to rinse off his toothbrush properly. My reminders to rinse his toothbrush didn't phase him.

"Joshua, why is there dried toothpaste on my and Mac's toothbrushes?" I asked at breakfast.

"Because I was trying them all out to see which colour I liked best," he answered simply.

"Please don't do that anymore." I moved closer to Joshua and placed my hand under his chin, looking directly into his eyes.

"Why?" Joshua gave me a half grin and tilted his head upwards.

"It's not sanitary."

"Oh, okay. What does that mean?"

"'Not sanitary' means it's not clean. 'Sanitary' means it's clean. In this case, you put something in your mouth that has also been in mine and Mac's mouths," I explained. "I'll need to buy everyone a new toothbrush, and we need to use our own toothbrushes at all times. Now, which colour worked best for you?"

"Purple!" he said.

I furrowed my eyebrows in confusion; none of our toothbrushes were purple.

Our bi-weekly meetings with Cassy and Rachael continued. Mac and I always asked if a family had selected Joshua for adoption, but their answers were always vague. We wanted to prepare Joshua as best as possible for any upcoming transition. Mac and I had yet to enrol in the level two foster parenting classes, some of which were on Fetal Alcohol Syndrome and Positive Parenting.

Joshua's family visits were routine and progressing fairly positively. Miranda had secured a part-time job at a local retail store near her house, with the potential for full-time hours, and Theodore was enrolled in an eight-week work apprenticeship course in carpentry. Both Miranda and Theodore were enthusiastic and hopeful that employment and training would help position them in a better place to gain back custody of their children.

One Saturday, Joshua and I awoke early to do a little shopping. We stopped at the children's store to suite him up with some summer clothing items and sandals. Next, we went to the local department store to buy new toothbrushes and select a birthday gift for his daycare friend. On our way home, we stopped at the Christian book store to pick up a couple of story books and gift items. I let Joshua look around the store on his own, reminding him not to touch anything. After a few minutes, Joshua quietly came over to me and grabbed my hand, pulling me over to the jewellery display.

"Can we buy a cross necklace for my mom?" he asked, pointing at the selection of cross necklaces.

"Sure! You can give it to your mom for Mother's Day next week," I said after thinking about it for a moment.

Joshua cheered and jumped up and down. A store clerk came over to ask us if we needed some assistance, and we asked her about the necklace. She retrieved the key for the display cabinet, and handed us the necklace: a simple but pretty sterling silver cross.

Once home, Joshua displayed all of the items and gifts we purchased for Mac to see. He was especially proud of the two gifts that Joshua had selected for his daycare friend and his mom. Mac cut the tags off of the new shorts and t-shirts and Joshua immediately picked out a matching set to wear for the remainder of the day.

They both went outside for some fresh air before supper. I asked Mac to walk over to the local recreation centre with Joshua to show him the swimming pool where he would be taking lessons on Mondays and Wednesdays from four-thirty to five-fifteen. When they got home, Joshua told me all about the slides and diving boards. He seemed excited about the lessons.

That Sunday, we made our weekly call to Joshua's mom. She was thrilled to hear that Joshua was enrolled in swimming lessons. Joshua also told his mom that he had a special present for her for Mother's Day. Miranda was excited to see Joshua at their next family visit and told him that he was thoughtful to buy her a present.

During our conversation together, she spoke about the challenges she and Theodore were having with their jobs. She talked about the set-backs they were experiencing with the Institute of Child Services. We prayed, and I continued to encourage Miranda to keep on with the battle. They had all come so far in this difficult journey. Now was the time to push back at the systems that weren't budging in order to move forward. Miranda needed an advocate who had been through the same journey, someone who had influence and experience to help them with upcoming legal hurdles, something I didn't possess. Fortunately, this person came along and began guiding Miranda and Theodore through the tangled process of undoing permanent placement orders. Though the process was extremely stressful and exhausting, between the lawyer and the family advocate's guidance Miranda's hope rekindled.

Joshua was off to his first swim lesson. The two of us walked over to the recreation centre. Once inside the building, the aroma of chlorine and the humidity in the air brought back fond memories of when my children attended swim lessons.

The swim instructor went through the roll call and then started the lesson. I sat with the other parents and guardians along the side of the pool and watched Joshua hesitatingly participate in the water activities. He wasn't ready to put his face or his head into the water and blow bubbles, even though the other children were laughing and bubbling over with joy, but he was splashing around and smiling.

We arrived home just before supper, just as Mac was pulling into the driveway.

"How was your first swimming lesson?" Mac asked with curiosity.

"I'm starving!" Joshua replied.

Mac looked at me, his eyebrows raised.

I shrugged. "He seemed to like splashing around with the other kids. The swimming instructor is very patient and encouraging. Joshua needs to overcome his fear of the water."

"Well, how about I come and watch one of your lessons, Joshua?"

"Yeah! You can see how I kick my legs!" Joshua said.

Joshua scarfed down his supper, laid his head down on the table, and didn't make a sound. Mac helped him through his bedtime routine earlier than usual; the sun was still out, but Joshua couldn't keep his eyes open. I listened to them them reading

"Noah's Ark." Joshua loved to read this book by memory, and, when he woke up the next morning, he asked if he could take it to daycare to read it to the other children.

"I think that is a fabulous idea!" I said.

Joshua grinned and put the book by the front door so he wouldn't forget it.

When I picked him up from daycare, Joshua and Marcy were on her driveway shooting a ball into a hockey net with hockey sticks. It was five-thirty, and he was the last one to be picked up.

"I'm so sorry for being late," I said as I walked up the driveway. "Traffic was heavy today."

"No problem," said Marcy. "Mr. Joshua did a great job reading to the kids at daycare today. I really like the way he added expression to the story! Now all of the other children want to read a book as well! Joshua really inspired them!"

"Good job, Joshua!" I smiled and high-fived his hand.

Joshua gave us a wide smile and responded, "Marcy said it's good to read and it helps us all get ready for kindergarten!"

We bid Marcy adieu and hustled home for supper, where we found Mac waiting on the driveway for us when we arrived home. Joshua asked Mac if he could ride his bike for awhile, which I thought would be a good idea while I made supper.

When I opened the door to call the boys in for supper, I couldn't see either of them. After a minute, Mac came up the driveway, a frown on his face.

"What's the matter?" I asked.

"Joshua isn't listening to me. I asked him to put his bike away and come inside for supper," Mac said.

"Maybe he's overtired," I said.

"Well, I'm so embarrassed! When I went to get him, he rode off on his bike yelling out, 'You're a bad man Mac, you're a bad man!' Some of the neighbours were outside and they could hear him!" Mac's face appeared to be a little bit red. He sat down on the bench beside the front door to gain composure.

I wanted to laugh; I could easily picture Joshua riding off on his bike wearing his helmet. Instead, I said, "I'll see if he'll listen to me. Why don't you wash up and pour us all some water to drink with supper?"

Mac nodded and went inside.

I went outside to find Joshua. I could see him sitting on his bike near the corner of the bay. I calmly walked over to him and said, "You need to listen with two ears, put your bike and helmet away, and apologize to Mac. I am going to count to—"

But, before I could start counting, Joshua stomped over to the house. I wondered why his mood had changed so drastically over the last half an hour. We would have to talk before bedtime.

That night, as I tucked Joshua into bed, I asked if something was bothering him.

"The kids at the daycare asked why I call you 'Sara' and not 'mom,' and why I don't call Mac 'dad.'" Joshua's mouth formed the biggest frown I had ever seen.

"What were you doing when they asked you?"

"We were making Mother's Day cards." His lips began to quiver.

"I see. Well, Joshua, you have a tummy mummy and daddy and a foster mom and dad."

"Why?"

I snuggled beside Joshua and held him close, speaking gently, carefully choosing my words. "Sometimes tummy mummies and daddies need some time to learn about being parents. A foster mom and dad take over until the tummy mummy and daddy are ready, so you are blessed with lots of people who love you."

"I made a Mother's Day card for you."

"That's awesome! How about you and I make another card for Miranda to go along with the cross necklace we bought for her for Mother's Day?"

"When should we make the card?"

"We can make it tomorrow, and you can give your gifts to your mom this week during your family visit!"

"Yay!"

I gave Joshua a big hug and a kiss. "Sleep tight, don't let the bed bugs bite!" I said as I closed his door.

Joshua arrived home from his next visit just as I was making individual pizzas for supper. He had been so excited to give his mom the cross necklace he picked out for her for Mother's Day, and I wanted to hear how it went.

"Yum, what smells so good?" he asked as he walked in the front door.

"Homemade pizza; everyone's favourite!" I called. "How was your visit?"

Joshua came running into the kitchen wrapping his arms around my waist, giving me a long hug. He looked up at me and replied, "Good!"

"Did your mom like the card you made and the cross necklace?" I asked.

"Yes!" was all he said. "Can I play cars until supper's ready?"

I nodded and sent him to the basement. Mac and I were never quite sure of what frame of mind Joshua would be when returning from a family visit, and I was relieved that it had seemed to go well.

The day of our next visit with Cassy and Rachael came, while Joshua was at his family visit. We discussed how things were going and possible dates for the upcoming courses Mac and I needed to complete as foster parents. They also told us our house would have a periodic inspection. The Institute needed to make sure our house was keeping up to date on safety conditions for Joshua. As well, we would need to set aside three hours of our time, which could be broken up into two sessions, to complete a comprehensive year-end review checklist and evaluation. Truth be told, both Mac and I were getting somewhat frustrated with the ongoing required training and continuous house checks, though we understood why they were essential. We complied with the requirements as best we could, however we couldn't find the time to take the next fostering course. I needed to complete report cards and Mac was travelling with his work, often requiring overtime hours. We were tired.

After Rachael left, Mac and I retreated to the kitchen to have a bite to eat and discuss what our next steps would be concerning foster parenting. I moved the food on my plate back and forth, not really interested in eating.

Mac silently watched me for a moment, then spoke. "What are you thinking?"

"I'm concerned that we won't be able find the time or the energy to take the next course required," I replied with dismay.

"Let's take it day by day. The most important issue here is to continue to nurture and parent Joshua and provide a loving home for him while he is here," Mac responded with sincerity.

———————

The long awaited and anticipated May long weekend was upon us. We looked forward to once again escaping the city limits to resort life. Even though there were many chores to do to prepare for the summer season, our spirits were lifted just thinking about our peaceful getaway. Mac and I needed a change in scenery to refresh our souls, and Joshua was looking forward to puttering along the shoreline to look for minnows and playing in the tree house. The three of us spent the weekend in the midst of soaking up the sun and securing the dock into the clear, cool water.

The following Saturday, we attended the water slide birthday party for Joshua's friend from daycare. Eight children soared down the water slide, their delightful screams and giggles rebounded across the pool. But, Joshua stood frozen at the bottom of the water slide, watching his friends glide down the slide and drop into the pool at the end of the slide with a big splash. Their encouraging words for him to join them couldn't convince him to climb the stairs to the top and have a go at it. I walked him up the stairs to the top of the water slide, but once there he sat down and hesitated. He wouldn't budge, even when the line up behind him was getting very long.

Finally, Nickolas, one of his daycare friends, sat down behind him and said, "I'll hold on to you."

Down they went. I could hear Joshua's shrieks as I made my way down the stairs, and I hoped they were happy ones. As I reached the bottom, I could see Joshua and Nickolas laughing while clambering out of the pool both yelling,

"Let's go again!" Joshua cheered.

My heart felt joy for Joshua. His friend helped him overcome a fear that had plagued him for the last year. Up and down the slide Joshua went, sometimes with Nickolas and sometimes on his own. The day was good. God bless Nickolas, and God bless friends!

CHAPTER TWENTY-THREE
summer sun, summer fun, soon to come

JUNE, THE MONTH when summer officially arrives, was also one of the busier months in the school year. Mac, Joshua, and Piper headed out to the cottage the first weekend in June so I could work on report cards at home. As well, it was my turn to volunteer on the sandwich train that Friday night. I anticipated a late night as the heat and humidity would likely bring many people to the train for food, water, comfort, and prayer.

Without distractions, I managed to complete most of the comments and grades needed for my students' report cards over the span of the weekend. The boys arrived home Sunday evening around seven. Joshua was hungry, so I made him a toasted-cheese sandwich. He seemed to be somewhat lethargic and picked away at his sandwich, most likely due to the heat and humidity. I asked him to speed it up a bit, as it was near bedtime and we all needed to get some sleep.

"I'm full," he said, putting down half his sandwich.

"Don't waste your food, a lot of poor people are hungry," I replied.

"There aren't any poor people in our city," Joshua replied, scrunching up his face.

"Yes, there are. While you were at the cottage, I volunteered to help on the sandwich train. We gave sandwiches to lots of hungry people, some whom didn't even have a place to go home to."

"Oh, where do they go?" Joshua sat up tall in his chair.

"Some sleep outside, some find a shelter, some need to go to the hospital because they get very sick, and others locate empty houses or buildings to stay in from protection from the elements." I retrieved a knife from the cutlery drawer and cut Joshua's sandwich into six long narrow pieces.

"What are elements?"

"Extremely hot or cold weather, rain and wind."

Joshua nodded. He picked up the sandwich strips one by one and slowly finished his meal. He was quiet during bedtime. I tucked him in and he never said a word, which was odd, as he usually had more than a few requests before finally settling down. He didn't even ask for a glass of water.

We all moved slowly the next morning. Mac was off to work while Joshua and I got ready for preschool and swimming lessons. Joshua continued to enjoy preschool, however, he would rather ride his bike than learn to swim.

"Do I *have* to go to swimming lessons?" Joshua dropped to the floor beside his bed, sat with his legs and arms crossed, and sulked.

"Yes, you do! It's an important life skill." I spoke firmly as I manoeuvred around him and pulled the quilt neatly over his bed.

"What's a life skill?" Joshua looked up at me from the floor.

"It's something you learn to do that can help you participate in every day life."

"Huh?"

"I'll give you an example. When we go to the cottage, we like to cool off in the lake, splashing around, using the flutter boards, and jumping off the dock or off the boat into the water. We have a lot of fun! It's important to learn how to swim so you can be safe in the water. Knowing how to do this is a life skill."

"Oh."

I reached down and pulled Joshua up to a standing position. "Please choose the clothes that you would like to wear today, Joshua."

I dropped Joshua off at preschool and decided to go for a run while I had a couple of child-free hours. I didn't mind the heat, I just needed to drink a lot of water post-run. Fifteen minutes into my run, it hit me: we had forgotten to call Miranda on Sunday. With Mac and Joshua at the lake and me in the city, our Sunday routine was disrupted. I was sure this was the reason for Joshua's mood this morning, and Miranda probably missed talking to him and learning of all the things he did over the week. I decided that Joshua and I would try to call her today when we got home from preschool.

Joshua seemed in good spirits after preschool. He had made a special Father's Day present during the arts and crafts session and said his teacher told the class to hide it in a safe place until Sunday. I asked him if he wanted to give it to Theodore, his biological father.

"No, I made it for Mac!" he said.

"Oh! Well, we can store it safely in your room somewhere," I said.

"It's breakable," Joshua warned.

"Good to know! We'll wrap it in a towel, then place it among your socks in the dresser drawer for extra padding." Joshua and I attempted to call Miranda before his swimming lesson. Miranda did not answer the call, the phone rang six times then disconnected.

At swimming lessons, I noticed Joshua was becoming a little bit more comfortable in the water, but he wasn't keeping up with the class. He watched as the other children moved forward on their flutter boards, kicking their legs. Joshua's teacher helped him with this activity, but as soon as she left his side to encourage the other children, he stopped doing it. I smiled at Joshua, he smiled back. The swimming lesson concluded and Joshua and I walked the half a block home in silence holding hands.

We celebrated Father's Day at the cottage with our family. It felt wonderful being out at the lake after so long away. We had many jobs to complete before our guests arrived Sunday, so on Saturday morning, we awoke early and got to work. Mac cut the lawn while I made a couple of sides for Sunday's family meal. After lunch, we launched the boat. Joshua was excited to sit with me in the open bow area while Mac drove the boat, cool water splashing our faces as we sped along down the lake.

Back at the cottage, Joshua, Mac, and I grabbed our bikes and rode to the public boat launch so we could pick up our truck and trailer. The hills were a bit of a challenge for Joshua to tackle. His five-year-old legs didn't have the strength to peddle up the hills, and we often stopped and walked up the steeper hills. Going down the hills, however, was quite thrilling: no pedalling needed!

When we arrived at the boat launch, Mac secured the bicycles in the back of the truck. Joshua noticed the playground, with children climbing on the structure and digging in the sand, located a short distance away from the parking lot and asked if he could play for a while. Mac and I watched as Joshua picked his way carefully to the play structure. He slid down the slide a few times and dug holes in the sand, but steered clear of the other children. It was hard to know what he was feeling and absorbing. Lately, he appeared to be unsure of social interactions and etiquette. Joshua needed to belong, but the more we tried to help him feel accepted, the more introverted he became. I noticed this behaviour was most prevalent when Joshua encountered families interacting with each other. He seemed to do fine at day care and preschool during free social playtime, but Joshua was well aware of how his family situation was different from that of his friends'. After about fifteen minutes, Joshua was tuckered out! We piled into the truck and drove back to the cottage, Joshua falling asleep within minutes.

Upon arriving at the cottage, Joshua's eyes fluttered open. Mac carried him down the stairs and plopped him on the couch. He continued to snore. After an hour,

Joshua woke up and made his way outside, where Mac was trimming the grass and I was reading on the lounger.

I asked Joshua if he would like to make a Father's Day card for his dad. I had brought some supplies along from a craft I'd done with my students: a card folded in the shape of a necktie, decorated with gumballs for golf balls and a ribbon at the top. I helped Joshua fold the paper and rewarded him with a gumball each time he completed a set of directions. Be that as it may, Joshua's mood was sullen, his movements slow and lacklustre.

"Joshua, you seem sad. Do you want to talk about anything?" I asked as we stuck a gumball onto the card.

"Do I have to give my dad this card?" Joshua asked.

"You don't have to, but I think he would like it."

"Can I go play in the sandbox?" he said, pushing the card aside.

"Sure!"

Joshua jumped down from his chair and ran off while I pondered his answer. I decided to ask Miranda during our next phone call if she could shed a little light on Joshua's relationship with Theodore. After all, Joshua didn't really know Theodore. They weren't part of each other's lives for quite some time, and a future relationship was uncertain at best.

Around twelve-thirty, Joshua and I tried to call Miranda, but only got through to a recorded message that the current mailbox was full. We gave it another try, however this time the phone rang two times then the call ended. I told Joshua that perhaps his mom was sleeping or running an errand and unable to answer the call.

———————

On Sunday afternoon, we got the deck ready for our family celebration. Joshua and Mac had swept the deck and set out the patio furniture, complete with a big bright umbrella to cover the table. The table itself would soon be filled with delicious snacks, appetizers, and drinks.

Joshua stood on the deck, watching with anticipation for vehicles to drive down the driveway.

He started to jump up and down when my dad arrived. "It's David, it's David!" he declared. Next, Tess and Tydon arrived.

"Do you like ice cream treats, Joshua?" Tess asked, as she and Tydon stepped onto the deck.

"Yes!" Joshua shouted.

Tydon opened the lid of the cooler he was carrying displaying a variety of cold treats. "We can eat these for dessert!" he said.

Joshua hugged Tydon for the first time since meeting him, and Tydon ruffled Joshua's hair, saying, "I like ice cream too."

By one-thirty, all nine family members had arrived with a side dish and snacks to contribute. We enjoyed cheerful conversation and our bellies were more than satisfied. Joshua uninhibitedly burst out with one of our favourite sayings, "We've got a lot of groceries in our tummies!" Our guests dissolved into laughter.

At six o'clock, our guests began to make the trip back to their homes, and by eight o'clock Mac, Joshua, and I were ready to head back to Rockport. Our drive was quiet, and we arrived home as the sun was setting.

"Joshua, look up at the sky. Look at all the brilliant beautiful colours!" I pointed out to Joshua as we got out of the car.

"How did it get like that?"

"The sun disappears below the horizon as the earth spins around," I said. "God created it like that. He made the heavens and the earth."

"Did God make everything, even the moon and the stars?"

"Yes, next time we're at the cottage, we can look at the night sky with the telescope in the loft and see the moon and stars close up."

Joshua kept his eyes on the sky as he walked up the driveway and suddenly tripped, falling face-first onto the pavement. He burst into tears. His knees and chin and wrists were scraped up a bit, but thankfully there was no blood. Mac picked him up and carried him to his room.

"You are sure getting heavy! How many hamburgers did you eat today? Ten?" Mac asked, trying to take Joshua's mind off his pain.

Joshua giggled and then sighed in contentment.

Joshua slept longer Monday morning, but Mac and I awoke as usual before seven. Mac left quietly after breakfast for work, and I planned and organized the week's activities on my calendar while sipping coffee. Joshua had a family visit this week on Tuesday, as well as his two regular swimming lessons today and Wednesday. Thursday was a big night for me, as my school had its year-end program and celebration that evening. The elementary students would perform either a song, dance, or creative production, as well as recite Bible verses as a large group for their friends and family. On Friday, we were hoping to go to the cottage and relax.

As I checked my emails, one in particular caught my eye. The Institute of Child Services sent us July dates for the courses they were requiring us to complete. Mac and I had totally forgotten about this. I quickly checked my calendar, as the dates that were listed seemed familiar. Sure enough, the dates clashed with our planned summer trip to Barrington to see Mac's parents. I wondered how we would be able to work around the conflict.

It wasn't until eleven in the morning that Joshua started the day. I made Joshua a hardy breakfast of a poached egg with cheese on top of an English muffin, a large glass of milk, and a bowl of green and purple grapes. By the time he finished eating and getting dressed, it was almost time for preschool. We filled his water bottle and packed a snack. Before we left, Joshua came bolting out of his bedroom with Mac's Father's Day gift in his hand. Over the busy weekend, we had forgotten to pack it up to take to the cottage so that Joshua could give it to Mac. We placed the gift on the kitchen table so that Mac would notice it at supper tonight.

While Joshua was at preschool, I baked banana bread loaves for us, my dad, and Joshua's family visit. I spread each with a thin layer of cream cheese icing. Before I knew it, it was time to pick Joshua up from preschool. He noticed the smell of the banana bread as soon as we got home.

"What smells so good?" he asked as we walked into the kitchen.

"I made banana bread for your family visit tomorrow."

"Can I have some now?"

"Of course! I made a loaf for us to eat as well. It'll give you energy for your swimming lesson."

I sliced a large piece of banana bread for Joshua to eat and I poured him a glass of apple juice.

"Can I take some juice to my visit too?"

"Yes, I can pack a carton of juice and some plastic glasses along with the loaf of banana bread."

"Yay!" Joshua stood up from his chair and clapped his hands together.

"Okay, eat up, we need to leave for swimming soon."

Joshua scarfed down his banana bread, and we headed off to his swimming lesson.

Mac was mowing the grass when Joshua and I arrived home from swimming. Joshua stayed outside and rode his bike around the bay while I made supper. When I called the boys inside, Mac noticed the tissue paper wrapped gift beside his plate immediately. He opened it up and was thrilled to find a blue hand print pressed onto a ceramic plate. On the back of the plate, it said "To Dad, Love Joshua."

"Did you make this at preschool?" Mac asked.

"Yeah!" Joshua replied with a wide smile.

"Wow, you are an amazing artist! I really like your gift! I'm going to hang it on the wall in the garage where I can see it everyday and keep it safe!"

After supper, Mac and Joshua ventured out to the garage to hang the special plate on the wall, where Mac had many other keepsakes from our daughters, as well as automobile memorabilia and trinkets.

The boys seemed to be out in the garage for quite a while, so I decided to peek in on them and see where they'd hung Joshua's gift. I found them looking at all the different knickknacks on the wall, Joshua wearing a headlamp, which he shined on each item. Joshua was asking all sorts of questions about everything in the garage, and was fully engaged with Mac's answers.

I didn't want to interrupt the conversation Mac and Joshua were caught up in, but it was getting late. I quickly snapped a couple of photos of Joshua and Mac together; we would put one photo by the ceramic plate on the garage wall and one in Joshua's photo album. I couldn't help but smile at how cute Joshua looked wearing the headlamp.

CHAPTER TWENTY-FOUR

The Ups and Downs of June

TUESDAY STARTED WITH an early morning thunder shower, waking all of us before six in the morning. Joshua played with the Lego for an hour before breakfast while Mac and I caught up on household chores, and I started a roast in the slow cooker. By seven-thirty, we all left home sporting raincoats. Joshua slid his rubber boots on and I grabbed an umbrella. I dropped Joshua off at daycare with the banana bread and apple juice for his family visit and headed off to school.

The rain continued off and on all day, making my classroom hot and sticky. I told my students that we would be rehearsing our song and performance on the stage in the gym for Thursday's celebration night. We would also be allowed to watch the other students practice their performances if we sat quietly. We had been practising for well over a month, and my students were well-prepared to perform their songs.

I arrived home by four-thirty, the aroma of the roast beef coming from the kitchen. I peeled potatoes and set them in a pot to boil and then mash. Mac arrived home around five-thirty and joined me in the kitchen.

"Did you get back to Rachael about the training sessions?" Mac asked as he poured himself a glass of sweet tea.

"No, I need to make it through to the end of June without distractions or added calendar events," I said, as I reached for dinner plates from the cupboard.

"Remember that we have a planned trip to Barrington; it's been a while since I've seen my parents," Mac said.

"I know, I miss them too," I said."

"I'll go ahead and book the hotel then; family's more important than taking a course."

"I agree. I'll email Rachael that this is not a good time for us to take their level two courses. Maybe we can catch up when life slows down a bit?"

"If you say so," Mac said sarcastically. "And when would that be?"

I shrugged my shoulders and went to grab the load of laundry out of the dryer to fold before supper. Mac finished setting the table for supper and mashed the potatoes.

Joshua walked through the front door around seven, half an hour later than usual. Mac and I had already eaten our supper. Joshua had a frown on his face, and his eyebrows were pinched.

"Would you like some roast beef and mashed potatoes?" Mac asked.

But Joshua eyes filled with tears. In between sobs and gasps for air, he spit out, "I want to go and live with Miranda."

As Joshua raised his arms and let his hands fall to his side in a motion of helplessness, Mac and I noticed markings in pen on his right hand.

"What is on your hand?" I asked.

"My mom wrote her new phone number on my hand. Her old phone doesn't work anymore and she wants you to call her."

"Alright. You and I will call her on Sunday afternoon," I said, squeezing his shoulder.

Joshua sat down at the kitchen table and nibbled on a small portion of beef, potatoes, and sugar snap peas.

"Did you give your dad his Father's Day card?" I asked.

Joshua nodded. "He was only at the visit for a little bit, I was late and he had to leave."

"Do you mean your driver was late picking you up from Marcy's?" Mac asked.

"Yeah, and everyone had to leave, so I didn't get to see them, but my mom stayed with me longer."

"I see. I'll do my best to find out what happened, okay?"

"Okay." Joshua sniffled, tears spilling down his cheeks again.

I got him ready for bed and we read a few bedtime stories. We prayed that his family would one day all be together forever. This settled him a bit, but he ended up crying himself to sleep.

We awoke Wednesday to another day of rain and somewhat cooler temperatures. Joshua played quietly in the recreation room and watched cartoons while I emailed the Institute of Child Services about the inconsistency of travel arrangements for Joshua's family visits and our inability to take the level two courses at this time.

That afternoon, Mac showed up by surprise to watch Joshua during his swimming lesson. Joshua spotted him immediately and waved, a huge smile on his face. After the swimming lesson, we walked home together, Mac and I each holding one of Joshua's hands. The challenges in our lives seemed to fade for the moment.

The night my students and I had been preparing for had finally arrived. My dad, Tess, Mac, and Joshua found seats in the gymnasium. I hustled to my classroom, where a few early bird students stood outside the classroom door waiting for my arrival. Soon my entire class was present and anxiously awaiting our curtain call. The boys looking very handsome in their black pants and white dress shirts, and the girls looking absolutely adorable in their elegant dresses.

At five minutes before seven we said a little prayer and made our way down the hallway to the entrance of the gymnasium. I peeked through the narrow windows on the door and saw that the gym was packed. The principal settled the crowd down and introduced the kindergarten class. My students walked on stage as rehearsed and then we all gave a little wave to the parents in the audience.

"All eyes looking at me," I said and waited for each student to look at me.

We performed two songs, one with actions and one with instruments. The students performed wonderfully, and the audience clapped and cheered when we finished. Happy and proud parents stood up from their chairs to show their delight.

At the end of the evening, the parents picked their children up from the classrooms, and enjoyed baked goods, coffee, and juice in the multi-purpose room. My own family quite enjoyed the show. Mac knew how much time and effort went into these types of programs; being the husband of a teacher for about twenty-eight years now, he had seen and heard it all.

On Friday morning, I received a call from the Institute of Child Services. The only answer they could give me about Joshua's late pick-up was that the driver himself was running late. They also informed me that Mac and I could take the level two courses online if we were unable to attend them in person. I thanked them for the information and hung up, much too tired to say or do anything else.

———————

We spent the weekend at the cottage. On Friday evening, the three of us eased into lawn chairs and relaxed. We noticed that hundreds of cocoons had appeared in the trees, under the eavestroughs, and just about anywhere and on anything that would house them. Baby caterpillars would soon be hatching if we didn't act soon to rid the property of this infestation. Mac made a batch of homemade insecticide out of dishwashing solution, water, and vinegar. He filled a couple of spray bottles and showed Joshua how to spray the cocoons.

The next morning, Joshua kept busy spraying the cocoons. Mac had explained that each cocoon must be thoroughly sprayed before the caterpillars hatched, and Joshua took this job seriously. With a blue cap on his head and some paper towel in his pocket, Joshua sprayed cocoon after cocoon with the spray bottle.

———————

The weekend passed quickly with going out on the boat and swimming by the dock. We also bumped into the Wilsons and made plans to get together with them later in July. Before we left for home on Sunday, Joshua and I called Miranda. She answered on the first ring, and Joshua eagerly told her all about his caterpillar hunting adventures.

After Joshua and Miranda talked for a while, Miranda and I had a heartfelt conversation. She disclosed that Theodore was not working anymore and that their finances were tight. Their phones had been disconnected, though she was able to find another one with a new carrier. She was frustrated with how their family visits were being handled. She felt that their family visit times were being disregarded. The children would show up late or not at all, and the Institute never told her the reasons why. I empathized with her and thought it best to just keep encouraging her to keep moving forward. I recited Isaiah 43:2, which often helped me when I found myself going through a difficult time:

When you go through deep waters, I will be with you. When you go through rivers of difficulty, you will not drown. When you walk through the fire of oppression, you will not be burned up; the flames will not consume you.

Even though we face many difficulties, God is with us and we should not give up. He will see us through our ordeals, and we will become stronger spiritually when we overcome adversity. I suggested that she keep track of the dates and times when her children were late to visits so that she she would have a record of the incidences if need be. Miranda thought this was a good idea and her mood improved. I then gave the phone back to Joshua to say goodbye until next time.

This final week of June passed by quickly, with preschool, swimming lessons, my and Mac's work schedules, and kindergarten orientation for next year's students.

On Wednesday morning, as I was just touching up my makeup in the bathroom, I heard a loud thump followed by crying coming from Joshua's room. I rushed down the hall and found Mac helping Joshua off of the floor, blood was oozing from the back of Joshua's head.

"What happened?" I asked as I fetched a towel from the linen closet. I brought it back and held it against Joshua's head while Mac sat him on the bed.

"Joshua was sitting on the edge of the bed. I stepped away to grab a t-shirt and the next thing I know, he's laying on the floor!" Mac replied with a puzzled look and frustration in his voice.

"He must have landed awkwardly on his head for it to be bleeding like this," I said.

The distance from the top of the bed to the floor was about two feet. Joshua must have dozed off, his body falling sideways onto the floor instead of the bed. I pulled back the towel. The bleeding stopped and Joshua started to laugh.

In spite of the hiccup, we all made it out the door on time, just a little frazzled. Mac took Joshua to Marcy's and I drove straight to work. I would pick Joshua up at the end of the school day. He wouldn't be attending his last day of preschool, as Mac was working out of town, and I was leading the orientation at school.

My day at school went well, but I was more than fatigued by four o'clock. Mac had texted me at lunch informing me that he would be working late and wouldn't be home until around eight o'clock. I picked up Joshua from Marcy's and then picked up burgers and fries from a near-by fast food restaurant. Joshua was thrilled and I was weary.

By the time Mac returned home from work, Joshua was sleeping. As we got ready for bed, he asked how kindergarten orientation went and how Joshua was feeling. I told him that there were enough kindergarten students enrolled to schedule two classes for next year, with sixteen students in each class. The principal had asked if I would consider full-time employment, and I had responded with a yes. I told Mac it would be nice to have extra income to help Tess with her schooling and accommodation when she moved to Foxpine in the fall.

"Yeah, that will definitely help, but we also need to keep in mind Joshua's ever-changing needs."

"I know. It's just for one year, and then we'll revisit employment options for my final teaching year before I retire."

"How is Joshua feeling?" Mac asked, as he sat down on the edge of the bed.

"He seems okay. He didn't mention his head hurt, but I picked up his favourite fast food for supper, so he was as happy as a pig in a mud puddle!"

"No kidding! Hopefully we'll have a better start tomorrow morning."

"Goodnight, Mac."

"Goodnight, Sara."

I buried my head into the soft down-feather pillow and barely heard Mac's goodnight. I was out like a light!

The last day of school was quiet. We had a staff meeting in the morning, and then I spent the afternoon re-organizing my classroom, removing anything that would take up space needed to accommodate my new students. I would unquestionably need to return to school at the end of August to prepare for the year.

When I picked Joshua up from Marcy's, she mentioned that Joshua had been complaining of a headache. As I was already planning on picking up a few groceries, I decided to stop by the walk-in clinic in the grocery store and have Joshua examined by a doctor. Joshua asked for a new Hot Wheels car, and I bought him one so he would have something to occupy him while the doctor examined his head.

The doctor on call went through a series of cognitive tests with Joshua and asked him a few questions. He then sterilized the wound, which was a tiny cut on the back of Joshua's head. The doctor didn't have concerns and said that the wound was healing nicely.

Joshua helped me unpack the groceries once we arrived home, then he scooted off to play cars in the basement, making car noises and crashing sounds. He was content, and I was relieved that his fall did not cause serious injury.

our second summer with Joshua

IN JULY, WE planned a three-week stay at the cottage. The Institute also sent me an email, which told me that Joshua would be attending a family feast during one weekend of our cottage trip. Cassy was arranging transportation to and from a park in the city. As she would be on holidays during that time, a different Institute worker would be picking up Joshua and two of his siblings between eight-thirty and nine o'clock on Sunday morning and dropping Joshua off back home at six in the evening. Mac and I decided that Joshua and I would come home for that weekend, so Joshua could see his family. Since Joshua would be with his family all day Sunday, I decided to make the best of the situation and go out to lunch with my dad after church.

That Sunday, I woke Joshua early and made him a big breakfast. We packed a travel bag for him for the day with sunscreen, a water bottle, a sun hat, and bug spray. His family was meeting at one of the more popular city parks, with barbecues, washroom facilities, and a children's park with slides, swings, and climbing structures. We had packed some cookies and juice for Joshua to bring, and he was excited to spend this time with his family. We were not sure of what kinds of food his family would be having, or if anything was needed, so we just sent items of Joshua's choice.

Joshua bounced up and down as we waited for his ride. Thirty minutes went by, and then another fifteen. I didn't have the new worker's phone number, so I wasn't able to contact her to find out what the delay was. Being Sunday, the Institute of Child Services main office would be closed. Joshua and I hopped into my car and went to church, leaving a note on the front door of our house to explain to the worker, if she showed up, where we were and why. My dad was waiting for me at church, and I was already late for the service. I would take Joshua to the park after church and hopefully find his family there.

Upon arriving at church, I found my dad waiting for me at the back. The pastor was well into his sermon, so we quickly found seats for the rest of the service. After church, I explained the situation to my dad and we decided we would meet up for an early supper if I couldn't find Joshua's family at the park.

Joshua and I drove to the city park and walked around for twenty minutes. It felt like eternity passed as we trudged by picnic tables filled with families that weren't Joshua's. It was already eighty-five degrees and not a cloud in sight! Finally, after standing near the playground for the next ten minutes, we saw Miranda and Theodore in the distance. They explained that they and the Institute had tried to move the location indoors, but hadn't been able to find a venue. Because of this, pick-up times for the children were delayed. Frustrated, I saw Joshua safe with his family and went home for a nap before meeting my dad.

It was nice to enjoy a meal prepared by someone else in one of my favourite bistros. My dad and I visited for a few hours before I needed to go home to greet Joshua from his outing.

Joshua arrived back at home on time, happy, and sweaty. I asked him who drove him to the house and he told me a taxi picked up him and his siblings. I wondered what would have happened if I hadn't been able to meet Joshua at home at six o'clock on the nose due to an emergency. I would have preferred that an adult could have walked him to the door or contacted me sometime during the day to confirm pick-up times. Joshua lay down on the floor by the front door. I took a closer look and noticed what appeared to be weeds stuck to his clothing and body.

"What happened to your clothes? They're covered with green weeds." I pulled a few sprigs of grass off of Joshua's shirt.

"We jumped into the lake."

"Oh dear, that's not a good lake to play in, it's filled with algae!"

"What's algae?" Joshua rolled onto his back and looked up at me, dragging out his words.

"Never mind, you need to get cleaned up before bedtime. Why did you jump into the lake in the first place?"

"We were so hot!" Joshua bellowed out as he staggered down the hallway toward the bathroom.

I sighed with exasperation. "Please throw your shorts and t-shirt down the laundry chute in the bathroom. I'll wash them right away."

Both Joshua and I fell asleep by nine o'clock that night and got up early the next morning so we could drive back to the cottage. We were just about ready to leave when the phone rang. The voice on the other end identified herself as Maria. She wanted to explain what happened. I tried to be amiable, but my tone came out indignant. I was frustrated with the way the situation was handled. I told her that I had made plans for the day and made a special trip back to the city so that Joshua could join his family for the feast. It would have been courteous of her to give me a call as soon as she knew she would be late. She offered no apology, just an excuse about the failed attempt to move the feast indoors, causing everything to get pushed back by an hour.

When we returned to the cottage, Mac could tell that my mood was off. I told him I would explain later; I just wanted to breath in the fresh air and relax on the deck, maybe read a book or go for a walk in the hills.

CHAPTER TWENTY-SIX
Where Did the Time Go?

BY THE TIME our vacation ended, it was mid-August. Joshua and I decided to go for a leisurely walk down the road Sunday afternoon while Mac loaded up the truck. Joshua noticed a path parallel to the ravine at the bottom of one of the larger, steeper hills we had strolled down.

"Can we explore the forest?"

"Do you mean the ravine?"

"That path down there through the trees."

"Sure, let's go and see where it leads!"

I held onto Joshua's hand as we made our way down the rocky and uneven path into the dried-up ravine. Mac and I had explored this area with our children when they were little, and we often found all sorts of little treasures on our adventures. One time we found buffalo horns, which now hung in our screened-in deck. Joshua was keen on finding a similar treasure.

We walked deep into the dense trees. The sun was obscured by the tall canopy, making our walk quiet and peaceful.

"Are there dinosaurs living in this forest?" Joshua asked. He pulled his hand out of mine and stopped to part the tree branches and peek through the leaves. I kept walking slowly along the entrenched path.

"I don't think so, they're extinct," I responded, smiling with amusement.

"Why do they stink?" Joshua asked, wrinkling his nose, which made me giggle.

"No, they're *extinct*, which means not alive anymore, but, you never know, keep your eyes peeled!"

Joshua hustled up to my side, staying close to me. I smiled at him, remembering his ferocious fun play with the dinosaurs and castle knights, and couldn't help myself from saying, "If we do see any, I hope they aren't hungry!"

Joshua stayed close to me for the entire hike through the ravine.

 When we arrived back at the cottage an hour later, Mac approached us.

"Where did you two go for so long? Did you climb up the hill behind the cottage?"

"No, we went into the forest to look for dinosaurs!" Joshua responded with excitement.

Mac furrowed his eyebrows and I said, "We walked through the ravine at the bottom of the hill with the steep incline."

"Oh, did you find any dinosaurs?" Mac replied, going along with the fun.

"No," Joshua said, his shoulders slumping.

On our way home Joshua pointed out the "forest" that we walked through for Mac to see, and Mac slowed the truck down to a crawl so we could all take one last look for dinosaurs.

On Monday morning, Mac returned to work and I checked our emails, finding a few from the Institute of Child Services about the second level course we needed to take; it was a progressive online training course with twelve modules starting in September. A feeling of irritation came over me. Mac and I were exasperated from the many demands that were placed upon our family. Though we understood that red-tape and paper work would accompany parenting Joshua, we had thought it would ease up after a year. Not so! As we moved forward, we required more training and more home inspections—in short, more time that we just didn't have.

 I took some time to respond to the emails. I made it clear that Mac and I would do our best to complete the training. However, with my full-time employment and Mac travelling with his job, we may require extended time to complete the course. In the back of my mind, though, I knew the course wouldn't make the top ten items on our "to do" list. We may not even get started with the training.

At our next visit with Cassy she informed us of a few changes to Joshua's family visits and the school that he would be attending. The Institute had found us child care near his kindergarten, which was in the same school as his preschool.. This was a bit of good news, as Joshua would be familiar and comfortable with the educational environment. Mac and I had requested that Joshua be allowed to attend school at the Christian academy where I worked, which had an after-school daycare program and suited our needs perfectly. The Institute denied our request, so Cassy committed to helping us find childcare for Joshua, even though she wasn't required to do so. As for family visits, they were being moved to Saturday afternoons from one until four. Mac and I found it interesting that the family visits were happening more frequently and for longer periods of time. As far as we knew, the Institute still considered Joshua to be a permanent ward of the state.

The next morning, I visited the school's website to have a look at the kindergarten school supply list. I printed off a copy and Joshua and I made a trip to the neighbourhood department store, where we shopped for every item on the list: markers, glue sticks, scissors, pencils, a blue plastic pencil box, crayons, erasers, a large scrapbook, and a pair of children's headphones. Next, we stopped at the sporting goods store for a backpack, indoor shoes, a matching water bottle, and a ball cap. We then made a quick trip to the discount shoe store to buy a pair of gym shoes for school and outdoor footwear as well.

Tess was planning on joining us for supper in the evening, and I decided to make her favourite meal, as she would be leaving for college at the end of the month, and it would be the last meal the four of us shared together.

Tess had found a basement suite to rent a short drive away from her college. We agreed to pay for the rent so that she could focus on her studies and not worry about finding a part-time job. We would be helping her move her belongings over the September long weekend and had booked a U-Haul trailer for the trip. I had also contacted the Institute of Child Services to request respite for Joshua for the weekend so that he wouldn't miss his Saturday visit. We also knew this trip wouldn't easily accommodate a five-year-old child.

Tess spent most of her spare time boxing up her personal items and clothing in preparation for her big move, Joshua accompanied me to my classroom to help me organize the classroom learning centres. We spent the next week and a half in my classroom from nine o'clock in the morning until around one o'clock in the afternoon. I was also able to do much needed planning and paper work while he played. Joshua had matured over the year and he played independently in the centres just as if this was his own kindergarten classroom. Once in a while, I would take a break to instruct, explain, and demonstrate how to use a particular learning centre, as some were more challenging than others. We brought sandwiches and snacks as well, just so he could get into the routine of what it may be like in his own kindergarten classroom. Joshua thoroughly enjoyed the time we spent together in my classroom at the academy and couldn't wait to start kindergarten in September!

CHAPTER TWENTY-SEVEN
Moving On

IN THE FINAL week of August, Mac needed to make a trip to Barrington to help his parents with a few house repairs and projects, and to spend precious one-to-one time with them. When he came home, Joshua bolted into his arms.

"Where were you for so long?"

"I went to visit my papa and mama," Mac said, hugging him tight.

"How come I couldn't come with you?"

"Well, I was busy helping my parents, and I'm sure you had lots of fun here in Rockport!"

"I helped Sara set up her kindergarten classroom!" Joshua said.

Later that evening Mac and I talked about his trip to Barrington. It was clear that we would need to spend more time with his parents and help them with a few repairs around their home. I reassured Mac that I was ready for work, so I would be able to return to Barrington with him the second weekend in September.

I put in a request with the Institute to take Joshua out of state, but it responded promptly with a firm "no." Instead, they requested an emergency meeting at our home on Monday afternoon at four o'clock. Mac and I were unsure of what to expect at this emergency meeting.

"Why do you think the Institute was in such a hurry to meet with us?" I asked Mac quietly, hoping he would have an answer.

Mac replied hesitantly, "Maybe we took to long to comply with the request to take the second course?"

We stood in silence, looking at each other straight-faced. "Do you think it's about something else?" I asked him.

"I don't know, it does seem odd that we would need an emergency meeting over a course," he said.

The day arrived. I felt my body freeze as the sound of the doorbell echoed throughout the house, sounding louder than usual. Mac opened the front door and invited Rachael and Cassy, as well as a supervisor into the house. We all made our way to the basement recreation room and sat down on the oversized sectional couch.

Rachael and Cassy shifted in their seats, unable to make eye contact with us, while Joshua played quietly with his Hot Wheels cars an earshot away. From the serious look on the supervisor's face, I realized the outcome of this meeting was already decided before we even began talking.

"We've decided to move Joshua to a new home," the supervisor said without hesitation, a blank look on her face.

I'll never forget the sound of the supervisor's voice. I couldn't speak. The pain in the back of my throat choked the breath and life out of me. Mac sat silently in utter disbelief.

"Can you tell us why?" I asked once I found my voice.

"Yes. We have found a family willing and eager to accept Joshua and two of his siblings into their home. We believe that this will be a positive way for the three youngest siblings to connect and build stronger relationships with each other. Joshua will be moved to the new family on Thursday."

"That doesn't give us much time to develop some kind of closure with Joshua or prepare him for a move," I stammered out my words.

"We understand. However, it's best to get all of the children settled before the school year starts. Sometimes moves are made quickly, it's just the way it goes," the supervisor responded. She rose from the couch, and Cassy and Rachael followed suit. All was said and done with no room for negotiation.

On Wednesday night after supper, we asked a few of our neighbours to join us on the front driveway for ice cream cones. The adults and Jasmine knew what the occasion was, but we thought it best for Joshua to just enjoy his ice cream with friends and neighbours. Joshua did not think twice or ask why we were eating ice cream cones together, he just enjoyed the moment, which was our intention.

That night, Mac and I both tucked Joshua into bed. He was pleased with the both of us taking turns reading a story book to him. Mac finished the story and closed the book.

I asked Joshua a question. "Joshua, do you remember when we prayed for you to be able to live with your family one day again?"

"Yeah," he responded, his eyes wide and his eyebrows tilted.

"Well," I continued, "God answered your prayer!"

Joshua sat up tall and blurted out, "I get to go and live with my mom?"

Mac intervened, "Wouldn't it be fun to be able to have brothers and sisters to play with and hang out with?"

Joshua looked at Mac and said, "Yes, and my mom too?"

I spoke. "Joshua, tomorrow you get to go and live with your brother Jake and your sister Anna in a new home. The three of you will visit your mom together."

"Oh," Joshua said. "Can I still I have visits with you?"

Mac answered, "We will give our phone number to the family you and your brother and sister will be living with, and you can call us anytime, maybe even all three of you can visit us."

"We will have to make sure it is fine with them first." I kissed Joshua on the forehead and reassured him that this was good news. "Joshua, this is the beginning of your family getting back together. We can get up early tomorrow and pack up all of your toys. Mac and I will pack your clothes, and Cassy will bring everything to your new home."

Joshua nodded his head slowly then fell asleep, exhausted after a long day.

A cab picked up Joshua on Thursday morning at seven-thirty. He didn't fully realize that he wouldn't be returning to our home. With his favourite teddy-bear in hand, Joshua hugged me and fist bumped Mac, then waved goodbye to the both of us. Joshua greeted the cab driver with a cordial "hello."

This little boy has matured and grown so much since he first came to live with us, I thought.

Tears formed in my eyes, and Mac held me close. "It's okay. He will be with family."

Mac and I packed up the remainder of his belongings when we returned home from work that day, and Cassy transported them to his new home. Then, Mac went out to the garage to putz around, and I took Piper for a walk, crying the entire time.

————————————

That weekend, I called Miranda.

"Hi, Miranda, it's Sara. How are you?"

"Could be better," she said. "Our lawyer is very determined and helpful, but it's really hard not knowing what's going to happen."

"Miranda..." I paused, gathering the courage for what I had to say. "I have something to tell you. The Institute has moved Joshua to a new foster home."

There was silence, and then I heard the sound of Miranda sobbing. Tears streamed down my face; I didn't know what say to comfort Miranda.

"They moved him a few days ago," I continued. "I wasn't sure if you were informed."

"No, I didn't know!" she cried.

I cringed and chose my words cautiously. "I don't have a lot of information about where he'll will be living, but we were told that Jake and Anna will be placed with him. Please keep fighting, no matter what! If the family they're placed with doesn't contact you, send them a note just as you did with us!"

"Can I still call you?" she asked.

"Yes, absolutely. We love Joshua just as much as you do."

"I can't believe it. Things were going so well. And even though we were battling for custody of our children, we knew that they all lived with loving families."

"I know. This doesn't change the fact that you need to move forward and stay strong! Your children will return home one day. Trust in Jesus."

We said goodbye and I hung up the phone with a heavy heart.

PART THREE
After Joshua

CHAPTER TWENTY-EIGHT
Empty Nest

WE SLOWLY ADJUSTED to how quiet our home had become. Full-time employment kept me very busy, and Mac travelled a bit more with his work. Tess made the college soccer team. Combined with her studies, she wasn't able to return home to visit very often, but Mac and I managed to travel to Foxpine now and then to catch a few of her games.

One night in early October, while serving on the sandwich train, I unexpectedly bumped into Miranda. I was startled, but happy to see her again. We gave each other a quick hug and sat down to chat. She was excited to tell me that proceedings were in progress for her children to return home under strict conditions: she and Theodore needed to find a bigger living space, and they were desperately searching for affordable housing. As well, one of them needed to find full-time employment to demonstrate financial capability and stability. She gave me her new phone number, and we agreed to keep in touch. I offered to help if she needed anything at all.

Two months later, close to Christmas, Miranda called me. She and Theodore were allowed to keep their children for the Christmas weekend. They hadn't found a larger home yet, however family visits had increased to a couple of times a week. Mac and I were very happy that their family would be together for the holiday and offered to drop off gifts and food.

––––––––––

The familiar tinging sound from my phone alerted my attention to a text, and I checked my phone: *Hi, Sara, it's Miranda. I'm so excited to tell you that we've found a place to live and I start my new job at the dollar store in one week! The children are being allowed to come home every weekend now, and if everything works out, the younger ones will return home permanently in July.*

I texted back immediately, *That's awesome! When are you moving into you knew place?*

In two days! she responded.

Sara: *Do you need help with anything?*

Miranda: *We're looking for a used washer and dryer in good working condition, that don't cost too much.*

Sara: *Mac and I will scan the used appliances section in the newspaper and check to see if there are any available at local garage sales. I'll call you if we find a set, and we can bring them over to your house in our truck.*

Miranda: *Thank you, that would be very helpful!*

Sara: *Got it!*

Four weeks later, on a warm Sunday afternoon, we delivered a washer and dryer set to the Sparrow family. A family from our church inherited a new set from their parents and were selling their older set. Mac and I decided to purchase the used pair as a house warming gift for Miranda and her family.

Miranda had asked if we would be able to visit with Joshua before he returned to his foster home, and we said yes. We hadn't seen him since last summer, and were very excited for the opportunity to see him again.

As we pulled up to the house, we saw Joshua standing at the end of the driveway waiting for us.

"Mac! Sara!" Joshua called as we got out of the truck. He scrambled towards us, crying and laughing all at once.

We knelt and caught him in our arms, smothering him with huge hugs. Tears began to drip down my face as well.

Miranda and Theodore came out of the house with the rest of the children and greeted us with hearty handshakes. Mac helped Theodore unload the washer and dryer and hook them up while Miranda gave us a tour of their home; she was proud of every square inch! It was obvious she had been hard at work, preparing the children's bedrooms and making the house comfortable for them. Mac and I were thrilled that this family, one we had gradually come to know as friends, were prospering as a family once again.

EPILOGUE

WE KEPT IN touch with the Sparrows over the years, through good times and bad. We helped where we could, lending a hand here and there, and we hosted Joshua and his siblings out at the cottage for a beach break two summers in a row.

Suddenly and without warning, a pandemic overtook society. The government mandated safety measures, stipulating citizens were not to socialize with anyone outside their family units. We were unable to have in person visits with anyone outside of our household, but managed to spend time talking with Joshua over the phone. Ironically, when Joshua lived with us, we would call his mom on Sunday afternoons to talk, but now Joshua and his mom were calling us once in a while to catch up with each other!

By the time the pandemic eased up and some restrictions were lifted, Joshua was eight years old. He spent a few weeks out at the cottage with us, a summer retreat from life in the city.

Perhaps only God knows how this story about people brought together to help and encourage each other, who respectfully developed friendships and genuine care for one another will move forward. This is a reminder that only God knows the end from the beginning. God creates divine appointments throughout our lives, even if we don't realize this truth.

ABOUT THE AUTHOR

TANA HOFF AND her husband of thirty-five years, Michael, live in Saskatchewan. Tana is a retired educator of more than thirty years. Tana and Mike have two grown children who reside in other provinces. For a period of time, they provided respite care for foster families and opened their home to a foster child.

Tana enjoys spending time at the cottage, writing, hiking and running, cycling, kayaking, and gardening. Sharing the gift of music with others has been extremely rewarding and has provided joy and countless blessings throughout her teaching career and through current musical opportunities.

A Boy Named Joshua: A Story of Belonging is Tana's second book. She was inspired to write this story from her extraordinary and memorable experiences as a foster mom.

Stories From Kindergarten, Tana's first book, was published in 2020. It chronicles her rewarding teaching career.

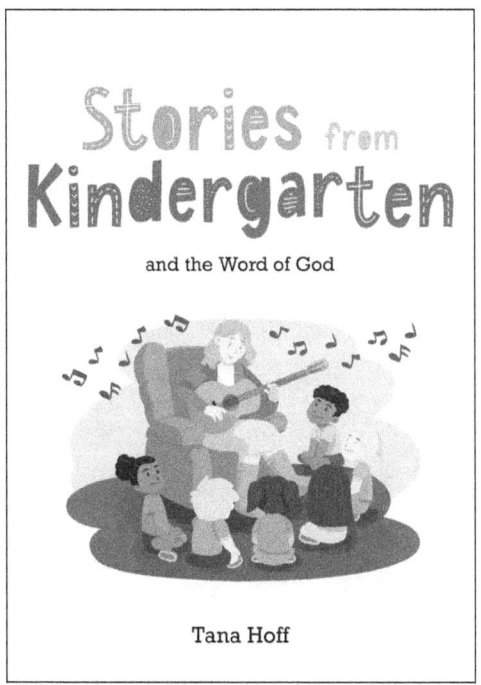

Stories from Kindergarten

and the Word of God

Tana Hoff

KINDERGARTEN IS AN island of its own.

Have you ever wondered what's behind the classroom door? Have you ever wondered why the noise level is pleasantly above the quieter levels of the Grade one to eight classrooms?

From the moment the students walk through the classroom door in the morning, to the time they depart at the end of the day, every single second is a teaching and learning moment, for both teacher and learner. As educators, how do we humble ourselves in a way that glorifies God? It's a lifelong learning journey. The stories in this book were lived and experienced through the eyes of a kindergarten teacher who had the honour and privilege to teach students over a thirty-year career.